Fear in First Gear

by

Karen C. Whalen

The Tow Truck Murder Mysteries

Cover Art by *The Wild Rose Press, Inc.*

The Wild Rose Press, Inc.
PO Box 708
Adams Basin, NY 14410-0708
Visit us at www.thewildrosepress.com

Publishing History
First Edition, 2025
Trade Paperback ISBN 978-1-5092-6166-6
Digital ISBN 978-1-5092-6167-3

The Tow Truck Murder Mysteries
Published in the United States of America

Dedication

To my husband and number-one fan, Tim

Chapter 1

"I need to find another shoeaholic like myself."

"Why's that?"

"The image." I drew up one high-heeled foot and looked over my shoulder to strike a pose.

Axle's gaze shot down the length of my blue jeans to my red stilettos. "Lose the heels today, Delaney Morran. Today's not the day."

Snow flurries hurtled in straight blinding lines across the parking lot where the sign for the autobody shop was barely visible above the door. Even though it was April, a blizzard had hit Spruce Ridge, a Colorado mountain town between Denver and Vail, and severe weather warnings beeped on our phones to alert travelers to the dangers on the mountain pass.

"You're right. For once." My parka was made with down feathers and my jeans were lined with flannel to keep me warm. The flimsy red shoes had to go.

"Say what?" He cupped a hand around one ear like he couldn't hear what I was saying. More like he couldn't believe what I was saying.

"You're right. You're right. Enjoy the moment." I dug around in the backseat and came up with a pair of rubber boots with thick soles. I braced my butt against the driver's seat and shucked off the heels, yanked on a pair of heavy wool socks, and jammed my feet into the boots. After tying my bootstrings, I stomped around in

1

the snow like a dog wearing booties for the first time. My new footwear weighed heavier on my feet than I was used to and left deep impressions in the snowpack.

I'd been called to a pile-up on I-70, a notorious stretch of mountain highway vulnerable to rockslides and avalanches. Right now, the issues were visibility and ice. Before the situation got any worse, the police had contacted emergency vehicles to extract stranded drivers and warn others to stay off the pass.

That a snowstorm hit in April was no surprise. That's the Rocky Mountains for you.

That I hauled cars for a living was a surprise. That's me for you.

Me, Delaney Morran. I drove a tow truck, just like the brawny, burly men who came to mind when you think of a tow truck driver. Only I was the opposite of brawny and burly. All five-foot-two of me. Or five-foot-five in high heels. I became known as the high-heeled tow truck driver after I showed up at my first tow in heels and the news went viral. I decided to embrace the image, which (for obvious reasons) set me apart from the other tow truck drivers in town.

Axle asked, "Why do you need to find another shoeaholic? What do you mean?" With his gloved fingers, Axle wiped the moisture off his phone, his constant companion. Large sloppy snowflakes stuck to the screen he'd just dried.

I sighed. "You're not always available to ride along, and I could use some help."

"Sorry, Delaney. I just got a text. Byron needs me today."

"See what I mean?" I told him.

At eighteen years old, Axle was younger than me by

ten years. He was an annoying teenager, but also a genius with anything mechanical. Since he was my best friend's cousin, that practically made him my cousin, too. Not only did he help me with tows, he rented my spare room and contributed to expenses. Axle didn't charge me anything when he came with me on tows, and I wasn't sure what I could afford to pay anyone else. My budget was tight. On top of that, I'd want to hire a car hauler who would agree to wear my trademark high heels and drive my self-loading tow truck painted red with the outline of a black stiletto on the door. I'd probably need to give up on that idea. No one would work for what little I could pay. And in heels. Not going to happen.

I hitched myself back up into my truck, tugged my knit cap snug over my ears, and pulled my leather driving gloves over my fingers. The smell of motor oil mixed with a woodsy scent clung to the upholstery, and I felt cocooned in the familiarity of the truck. I loved my amazing Fulcan Xtruder with its integrated lift. My attachment to the self-loader was easy to explain; it had been my dad's and I felt connected with him when I drove it. As a bonus, the elevated cab had a high clearance allowing me to see the road ahead much easier than my personal vehicle did—a Fiat, which was not the best for winter driving. My truck gave me confidence.

After Axle trudged through the snow into the autobody shop, I aimed my truck in the direction of I-70 to ascend the Divide. By the time I reached the accident scene, most of the vehicles had been removed already and the few that remained were busted up beyond make and model recognition. Whoever arrived first got the job, and it was competitive.

"Hello, there!" I waved out my window at Tanner

Utley. He gave me a solemn nod before continuing to operate the winch on his powerful black flatbed to extract a sedan with a smashed front end. This tow man was the one who showed me how to operate my self-loader, and he was the best vehicle recovery agent in town. I'd had a huge crush on him, and we'd dated for a while not too long ago.

One of the state troopers came alongside my driver's door. "Hi, Delaney. Can you drive up County Road 350? We need to make sure all the vehicles are off Clarkson Pass before shutting the snow gates."

"Of course. I'll go right now." I rolled my truck slowly past the accident scene. It wasn't a wasted trip for me after all; I was about to perform an essential service. Closing highways was not easy, and my help was needed to keep vehicles off the dangerous road until the weather cleared.

Leaving everyone behind, I took the exit toward the summit. Under normal conditions, the top of the road opened the view for hundreds of miles, and the harsh call of the Steller's jay echoed along the ridge, but not today. When I reached the top of the pass, snow sped sideways across the pavement, covering the painted lane lines and forming drifts, making the world a monochromatic white. The sound of ice pelts blasting against the roof of the truck grated on my already tingling nerves, somehow more agitating than a car alarm. Even though it was afternoon, I flipped on the bright headlight beams.

I had the illusion of going uphill but felt the truck gaining speed, so I applied the brakes and immediately fishtailed on ice. That weightless, powerless feeling made my stomach plunge.

Crap.

I moved my foot from the pedal to steady the truck, and the tires caught hold of the road. I must have overtaken the summit and was now on the descent. There were tall plow markers on the pavement's edge but no railings, so my fear kicked up another notch. I dropped into first gear to avoid more braking and continued at a crawl. Riding the brakes down a pass was never a good idea. The highway patrol would not let anyone enter the road behind me, so I didn't have to worry about someone coming up on my tailgate. I could go as slowly as I wanted by staying in low gear.

The sun broke through the flurries and lit up the snow like diamonds. There was nothing prettier than white-covered mountain peaks and snow-draped blue spruces peeking out of low clouds, and I took in a deep breath of the cold mountain air infused with the scent of pine that made its way inside the cab. Then gray overtook the sky and the mountains disappeared from view once more. For a few moments, the whiteout enveloped my truck, and I sensed more than saw a curve in the road.

Suddenly the wind blew in a different direction and a clear spot opened up in front of me. My headlights illuminated a vehicle on the shoulder. Since I was on the curve, the truck faced the car and the beams of my headlights landed on a woman in the driver's seat, her head turned toward the window. She didn't blink away. Her skin was white, her mouth slack, and her eyes open and dull, as if out of focus. She had an utter lack of expression.

I gasped and pressed a hand to my mouth.

Double crap.

I'd automatically turned the wheel and was already

around the curve, so I found a straight grade to pull a U-turn. The wind constantly shifted the snow, and visibility was once again limited to a few feet. With flurries coming from all directions, I inched back toward the summit but felt like I had driven past the woman, so I reversed direction again. This time I knew I'd driven too far because I was back on the downhill side of the pass, but I was disoriented and couldn't remember the exact spot where I'd seen the car. Should I try going farther down or return to the top? I decided to give it another try and hung a u-ey to make the trip back and forth one more time.

Frustrated, I brought my truck to a stop in the middle of the road and yanked off one glove. I keyed in 9-1-1 on my cell but didn't hear a ring. No bars, no service, no help. I was chilled down to my toes.

The snow stuck to my windshield.

I could hardly distinguish the road.

What good would it do to search any further? The woman was dead. I'd bet my best rachet wrench on it.

A tree branch fell with a loud *C-C-R-R-A-C-K*, partly blocking the road behind me and almost sending me out of my skin. Goosebumps raced across my arms, and my heart pounded so hard my brain cells rattled around. That's why I headed down the pass. I wasn't thinking straight. Trees were toppling over. The road was dangerous. The car on the side of the road might now be buried in snow. Besides, the woman was dead. There was nothing I could do to save her. And even if I went back and found her vehicle, she was beyond help.

The final descent was slow with the truck in first gear. My fingers ached from gripping the wheel, and my heart jolted with each gust of wind. Vehicles skidded off the road more often than you would think, and I didn't want one more—my own truck—to go over the cliff.

My dad was the victim of a fatal car crash himself—a hit and run off I-70.

When my dad, Del Morran, died, I felt abandoned, which made no sense because I didn't even know him. I'm twenty-eight now, and my parents divorced when I was seven. My only contact with Dad had been impersonal birthday cards and Christmas gifts. Del Morran had not left me many memories, but he did leave me his name and his Irish red hair…and his tow truck. Somehow driving his self-loader gave me a déjà vu kind of feeling, a bond I never felt when he was alive.

For a moment I imagined Dad sitting next to me. I could almost hear a whisper in my ear that I was going to make it down the pass just fine.

I shook myself. Good God. This storm was creeping me out.

Finally, I drove out of the blizzard and left the heavy snowfall behind. The weather was not as bad in town, only a light drizzle, as I coasted into the parking lot at Roasters on the Ridge. There was sure to be phone service here. Warmth and coffee would be good, too.

As I walked through the door of the charming coffee shop, Kristen rushed up to me, her gray eyes shining. "Delaney, I'm so glad you're here. One of the judges stopped by to tell me I'm getting a high rating. I think I'm in the running for the number one spot. I'm making free drinks for everyone." She turned on her heel, her long, brown hair swishing out in an arc as she headed back toward the espresso machine. A well of affection for my friend rose in my chest. She deserved to win the Top Ranked Restaurant award in the coffee shop category. She's a roast master, a purist who roasts her own beans and runs the café with the highest of standards.

In the corner, Axle was propped on a stool in front of a bass drum next to a snare and a couple of cymbals. In addition to being a genius auto mechanic, he was an aspiring musician. He must've come straight here after work at the autobody shop. He tossed a drumstick in the air and tried to catch it, but it clattered to the floor. He snatched the stick from between his feet in one quick motion and yelled, "Hey, Delaney, you back from that accident?" Before I could answer, he clicked the two drumsticks together with a *tap-tappety-tap* and went on, "Are you here for our music? I didn't tell you how sublime the band was last night. Everybody thinks we're awesome." Axle beat the snare, *rat-a-tat ratta-tatta rat-a-tat*.

The other musicians on the makeshift stage laughed at Axle. Kristen called out, "Who wants what to drink?" and a loud whoosh erupted from the espresso machine. Axle trod the drum pedal, *boom-bah-boom*, and repeatedly hit the cymbal with crash after crash.

The stress of it all hit me, like the slamming of brakes, and a vibration went through my body. Expecting my knees to buckle at any time, I tossed my hat and gloves on a table and collapsed onto a chair. I needed to shake off this punch to my gut.

My eyes went to the quaint signs—"Coffee makes everything possible" and "Humanity runs on coffee." Antique skis and poles, snowshoes, and ski boots decorated the walls. Distressed-wooden shelves held beans, mugs, and syrups. Two teens sipped lattes at the table near the window. A couple of middle-aged women nursed hot drinks with matching books in front of them—probably a book club. The band paused in their warmup and I enjoyed the unexpected respite. The aroma of the brewing coffee and the low voices of everyone present provided a sense of calm, but my shoulders were tight and my stomach was still churned up.

As she approached me with my drink, a questioning gaze appeared on Kristen's face. "What's the matter, Delaney? Are you all right?"

I shook my head and plucked a double espresso from her grasp. "Are you ready for this?" I paused, my throat tightening at the memory, then blurted out, "I saw a dead woman."

All eyes shifted toward me. The teens allowed me a *so-what* stare. The band members exchanged looks, and Kristen pulled in a sharp intake of breath.

"Again?" Axle's gaze went to the coffee shop ceiling.

"Yes."

"In the car crash?" His eyes narrowed ever so slightly. "The one you got called to on the pass?" He'd been with me when I received the call. That felt like hours ago.

"No, I didn't even work the crash. State Patrol sent me over Clarkson Pass and I saw a dead woman."

He said, "You're joking, right?"

"Wrong." I clutched my coffee cup to my chest. "She was just sitting there in her car. Dead. D-e-a-d. It was totally ick."

"Where on the pass?"

"I don't know."

"What kind of car?"

"I don't know."

"You always know the make of the car."

"It was covered with snow!" I rolled my eyes.

"Jeez, don't get mad."

"I'm not!" I had to cringe at my crabby tone.

"Did you call 9-1-1?"

"Doing that now." I set my cup down and checked my cell; it had bars. I punched in the number for the city police department since the pass was on this side of city limits. I left a message for Officer Zachariah Bowers, whom I knew well, to return my call. "Done," I told Axle.

He went back to his drums with a *dumba-badump*.

I really wished Axle had been with me on the pass. He may be a pain in the heinie, but he was a great wingman. As Kristen's cousin, he had her same gray eyes and thick dark hair, only his hair was cropped short and continuously tousled when not covered by a knit beanie. Kristen owned Roasters and leased the entire building that included the two apartments on the second floor. Axle and I lived in the apartment across the landing from Kristen's.

"Delaney." Kristen shook my elbow. "Tell me what happened. Did you stop to check on the woman?"

My gaze went to her kind face. "No, I didn't stop. I was so shocked I kept going." When I saw my friend's lips thin, I flushed with self-reproach and knew my cheeks were crimson from my red-headed tendency to blush. "I tried to go back and find her car, but I was so disoriented I just gave up and came here."

Kris sank into the chair across the table. "Are you sure the woman you saw was dead?"

I nodded, staring into my coffee mug. A person with an utter lack of expression like that had to be dead. But why hadn't I tried harder to go back and find the car? Should I have searched one more time? Had the icy road freaked me out?

"I'm sorry." She rubbed my shoulder, concern evident on her face. "So, another body? How many does this make?"

"Too many."

"You've been through an ordeal. Relax and drink your coffee. Try to think about something else and I'll check back with you in a sec." She stood and went around to the other tables, greeting each customer.

My cell rang with a return call from the Spruce Ridge police officer. I couldn't give Zach the mile marker, the make of car, or anything else. He kept asking for specifics that I was unable to provide, and I could tell he was skeptical. Even I started to doubt my own story, hearing it like this. He reminded me that the road had been closed. Besides, whether the road was open or not, it was unlikely anyone could get up the mountain now. Not until the weather cleared, and then the plows had to move the snow, but he would let the department know. I was not to worry; they would figure it out. But right now, the high winds had caused several semis to tip over. There were reports of windshields popping out of vehicles. All the officers were out on patrol, but one of them would make an attempt to check the area, although it could take a while.

So I guess my report of a dead body was low priority.

After I hung up, I gazed out the coffee shop window into a bleak wet landscape. No one around me seemed upset. They'd all gone back to doing whatever they were doing before I'd walked in. Kristen waded among the tables, passing out drinks, consumed by the city-wide contest for the Top Ranked Restaurant. Axle and his buddies played their instruments, preoccupied with breaking into the music business so they could escape their regular jobs. They were all going about as normal, even working toward their dreams.

As for me, did I have any dreams? Other than hauling cars without damaging any? Making enough money to pay the bills? Believe it or not, neither of those goals was easy. For me, anyway.

Guy, the part-time college student and full-time barista, came over to spritz the table next to me with vinegar water. He backed up, his shoe hitting the leg of my chair. "Oh, you're still here." He gave me a sympathetic look. "I heard what you said about a dead body."

"Yes?" My eyes dampened.

"Kristen has her restaurant competition and Axle has his band, but poor you, you have nothing. Is that why you need to report another body? Is that why you made that dramatic announcement?" He made a tsking sound with his tongue. "Those high heels don't bring you enough attention?"

What a twist of the knife.

I had no idea what to say. Seriously! I wasn't even wearing heels right now.

Guy used to be my favorite barista, but not at the moment.

I snatched up my hat and gloves and scraped my chair back. I stepped outside, letting the door slam shut behind me. My shoulders hunched up as I buttoned my parka against the cold. I had a bad feeling no one believed me, other than Kristen who always had my back. She'd believe me if I said I'd seen a man from Mars on the mountain. Granted, me finding yet another dead body was a bit farfetched. I got that. What were the odds?

I raised my arms to the sky. "Why me? Why me? Why do I always have to find the body?"

Snowflakes swirling around the nearly empty parking lot whipped my voice away.

Chapter 2

The sun peeked through the gap in my bedroom curtain. There were no sounds of sleet against the windowpanes; instead, traffic noises blared from the busy intersection at the corner.

Nudging myself out of bed, I stretched my arms over my head, took a deep breath, and went to the window. The City of Spruce Ridge sat in the middle of a wide valley surrounded by rising peaks that reflected the morning sun. Today, daybreak was clear and bright, and the view took my breath away like it always did.

My head was throbbing, screaming for caffeine, so I went to the kitchen to start the coffeemaker. After Boss, Axle's Rottweiler, whined and stared at his food bowl, I loaded him up with kibble. While the coffee brewed, I took a long shower.

I can't brush my long curly hair when it's dry because the curls will turn to frizz. My hair needs to be combed when wet, so after shampooing, I applied conditioner and ran a wide-toothed comb down its length. After rinsing under the streaming hot water, I stepped out and pressed a towel against the wet strands that fell down to the middle of my back. I let my locks air-dry while I dressed in a pair of jeans and a green turtleneck sweater, then twisted my hair into a braid.

By the time I was ready, Axle was in the kitchen

with a bowl of soggy cereal.

"Morning, Ax. You need a ride to work today?" I gave him a flick to the ear. He grunted in reply and rubbed the side of his head. "Is that a yes or a no?" I asked.

"That's a no." My li'l cuz—that's what I called him—was easy to be around when he spoke only three words at a time.

"Okay, then. Whatever you say."

After two cups of coffee, my headache disappeared. Axle walked Boss over to the park across the street and then left for work, so I retrieved my phone from the charger and called Zach.

This city police officer is an all-round good guy with a high moral code. He had a prominent chin, handlebar mustache, premature salt and pepper hair although in his thirties, and a serious crush on Kristen. She was serious back at him, and they were "courting," whatever that means. I think it signified they're dating exclusively.

"Is the pass open?" I asked when I reached him.

He answered, "I have bad news. There's been an avalanche on Clarkson Pass. No access. County Road 350 is blocked."

"Oh, no." I placed a hand over my heart. "An avalanche! Was anyone hurt?"

"No reports of injuries."

I tugged the kitchen blinds open to look out again. "It's nice here this morning."

"You know the weather can be completely different at the summit."

"Yeah. Any news about the woman I saw?"

"Are you sure the whiteout didn't cause you to see things?"

I gulped, "What?" His words made my stomach clench.

"Hallucinations can appear during sensory deprivation, like when you can't see anything but white. Happens to skiers sometimes."

"I didn't hallucinate." I could sense Zach giving me one of his doubting looks over the phone. "Someone will check the area as soon as the road opens?"

"Of course."

I choked out the words "Thank you" and disconnected.

I could barely pull air into my lungs. Zach didn't believe me. Nobody but Kristen seemed to be taking me seriously. Yes, I wore high heels on tows, when it was safe to do so, and maybe I'm not the best tow truck driver in town, but I know what I saw. A dead woman in a parked car. And now an avalanche made it impossible to confirm or deny.

I did see it, right? Yes, yes, I did.

But it was only one day later and already her face was fading from my memory. Were her eyes brown or blue? Her hair color? I couldn't remember. Did I even notice those details? Probably not. I do recall her white complexion. Her vacant expression. I did catch a glimpse of that.

I hurried along the hallway to my bedroom and rifled through my closet for my old whiteboard and dry erase markers from college days. Writing my thoughts on the board would help me organize my mind and recall everything, I hoped. There wasn't much to go on. Of course I didn't have a photo of the victim, no name, no facts, so I drew a stick figure. Then a cartoonish diagram of a car with a jagged arrow pointing from the figure to the car. I added these questions:

Was it a car accident?

Was it a stall?

Was it weather related?

How did she die?

Did she fall asleep and freeze to death?

Did she have a heart attack or stroke?

Who was she?

I positioned the board on the kitchen counter and stepped back to study what I'd written. The car didn't appear smashed up, so a car accident didn't look as likely to me. That was my initial impression, anyway. Maybe it was a stall. Or she could have pulled off because of the storm and froze to death, but she wasn't in a sleep state with those wide open eyes. And as far as a stroke or heart attack—she looked too young for that.

What if there was foul play? That wasn't much of a stretch for me to consider. Look who's talking here—me, remember? I've found other bodies and all of them were homicides. I mean, if someone wanted to get rid of a corpse, leaving it abandoned in a snowstorm would be one way to do it.

Was there a murderer out there? Did someone kill that poor woman? Who was she? Who killed her? How? Why?

Would the answers come to me if I contemplated the whiteboard long enough? That was what the cops did in television crime dramas, but I'm not sure it was all that helpful. Perhaps if I had more to write on the board.

Like a name, at least. The woman deserved a name. And definitely more answers. It seemed wrong not to find out what happened. I'd left her on the pass; I'd driven away to safety. I owed her. Besides, I was doing my duty as a citizen by asking questions. She had a right to be taken seriously and so did I.

The phone rang and I jumped. A name popped up on the caller ID. It was Zach, so I answered, "Is the pass cleared already?"

"No, road's still closed. But I did some checking, and there's a weather cam at the bottom of County Road 350. There used to be a weather station there years ago, and now there's a webcam operated remotely."

"Did the video show something?"

"No other vehicles came down that canyon other than your truck. I guess drivers didn't want to navigate the pass in that bad weather. Smart."

"Well, except for that woman."

He paused for a couple of beats. "Okay."

"How well does the camera work in a snowstorm?"

"NOAA has sophisticated equipment, Delaney. I'm confident no one drove that road except for you."

"How much of the video did you look at?"

"About three hours, up until I spotted your truck. The recording is real-time, but I was able to fast forward through it pretty quick."

"So, no one came down the pass during the three hours before I did. What about earlier than that?"

He sighed. "I'll do some more checking and get back to you. No promises as to how soon I'll get to it."

We disconnected.

I slid my arms into a fleece jacket, hiked my purse onto my shoulder, and thundered down the stairs to the parking lot. Despite the freezing weather the day before, on this April morning spring was in the air and the sun had melted any snow that had accumulated. Over the last week, buds had started to sprout on the trees, giving them a hazy green aura.

I zipped over to the Clear Creek County Sheriff's Department in my Fiat, arriving in minutes. Nothing is very far in this small town. The Spruce Ridge City Police Department, where Zach worked, investigated traffic accident deaths, but all other deaths, such as homicides, suicides, or unattended fatalities, were investigated by the county sheriffs because, I was told, they were better equipped and trained.

And one particular county sheriff was well known to me. Sheriff Ephraim Lopez. Talking to Ephraim was the obvious next step, for many reasons—like, because he and I were dating.

I entered the sheriff's station in a modern office building with big windows and lots of natural light. Pristine and quiet and new. The duty clerk ushered me into Ephraim's office. His desk, a swivel chair, and two visitors' chairs crowded the space. Framed citizen awards and photos with dignitaries hung lopsided on the wall.

Ephraim stood up with a broad smile. "Good morning, Delaney." Dimples appeared in his cheeks.

The sheriff is taller than me by ten inches and older than me by ten years. He has the bronze complexion of his Mexican heritage, with chocolate brown eyes, long dark eyelashes, and thick black hair, and his uniform hinted at serious muscles underneath. My nose picked up a whiff of his scent, like citrus, jasmine, and musk— clean and fresh and appealing. He was such a gorgeous lawman in his cowboy hat and badge that he took my breath away.

"Morning, Ephraim." I dropped into a visitor's chair.

Ephraim sat back down. "Why'd you come by? Are we still on for tonight?" The two of us have an undefined relationship. Yes, we date, but I never called him my boyfriend, and that sounded lame anyway. After all, he's thirty-nine years old and divorced. I'm twenty-eight and never married. At our ages, boyfriend-girlfriend labels seemed immature.

"Counting on it. My place. Six-thirty." I ran my hand down the braid resting over my right shoulder. "Did you hear I reported a dead body on County Road 350?"

His jaw dropped. "No. What? Tell me about it."

I recited the scant details, then asked, "Can you check to see if a missing person's report has been filed?"

"Sure, I can do that." He seemed to believe me, but then he'd better or there would be a serious dent in that undefined relationship. "It happened yesterday. Why did you wait until today to let me know?"

"Well, I called Zach and he said someone on patrol would check the pass, but then the avalanche happened—" I paused for emphasis "—and then I got to thinking, what if there's a crime involved?"

"What are you saying? There's been a homicide?"

"Maybe." I crossed my legs and stared down at the black stilettos I'd put on today. Black, for being taken seriously. "What if someone left her corpse in that car hoping the snowstorm would cover up the evidence?"

"Did you see a bullet wound? Signs of violence? Other indications?"

I met his gaze. "No. Just a feeling." I had that kind of bad luck. The kind where I find homicide victims. Bad luck followed me around. But then, at least I was luckier than the woman in the car. I was alive. The poor woman was dead. I'm almost positive. Even if she wasn't then, she is now in the aftermath of an avalanche. The road had been closed after the last vehicle came through, and that was mine. Her car never made it down. Not that she could've driven it. She was dead! Someone needed to do something!

"You know, whenever you see anything suspicious, you need to contact the authorities immediately." He reached across the desk and took my hand in his, lacing his fingers with mine. His strong hand was reassuring, but his words made me feel chastised.

"There was no cell service at the summit, but I called Zach as soon as I got to Spruce Ridge. Plus, I thought at first it could be weather related. I didn't immediately think it was suspicious. And I'm not really sure I do now, but I thought you might want to look into it, just in case." I cursed my pale complexion as my cheeks grew warm. If I'd been able to report the woman right then and there instead of leaving the scene, the cops would've arrived before the avalanche. Darn that no-cell zone. Next time, if there's any possible way, I'd make that call sooner.

Next time? Did you catch that? Hardy har har.

"Why didn't you call me first?"

"This side of the summit is within city limits, so I thought of Zach. 9-1-1 calls go to the city police anyway, so I figured I'd call him directly."

"Okay." He let go of my hand. "I need to get to a meeting. Sorry, Delaney, but I'm late already."

We both rose from our chairs. He stepped back so I could precede him down the hallway, and he walked me to my car.

On the way home, I stopped at the grocery store to pick up ingredients for dinner. When I opened the door to my apartment, Boss tried to dart outside, but I blocked him with my legs and shoved the door closed. He'd been trying to escape lately, and it had me worried.

I set the grocery bags on the counter. "Boss, I'll take you for a walk later." The Rottweiler sniffed the air, then flopped at my feet with his muzzle in his paws.

After I'd put the meat in the fridge, my cell rang with a call for a tow. Although my customer said there was no rush, that he only wanted his car moved across town sometime today, I patted the *Rottie* goodbye and hightailed it in my Fiat over to Oberly Motors for my tow truck.

After my dad's death, Byron Oberly had bought Dad's autobody shop. I'd inherited the tow truck; Byron had purchased the business. He and I became good friends, and I rented the secure fenced corner of his lot for impound space. That was where I stored my truck. Axle worked for Byron as an auto mechanic, so I often dropped off Axle in the morning, and sometimes I picked up Axle at the end of the day. That I got a chance to see Byron all the time was a bonus.

The whine of hydraulics blasted from the first auto bay, followed by the boom of heavy equipment hitting the ground. I ducked under the overhead door to the smell of motor oil and rubber tires. Byron looked out from under the hood of a Honda CRV, front-wheel drive, and Axle nodded from the second auto bay where a Dodge Viper, rear-wheel drive, hung suspended from a lift. I patted myself on the back for knowing the make and drivetrain, something I'd had to learn in this business.

"Hi, Old Man." I called Byron Old Man the same way I called Axle my l'il cuz. Byron was pushing fifty or even sixty, and heavyset, always in coveralls with a rag in the pocket.

"Hey, Delaney. Good ta see ya on this beautiful Wednesday mornin'." He gave me a gap-toothed smile.

"It is a nice day, isn't it? Especially compared to yesterday. Did you hear about the avalanche?"

"Sure, sure. It was all over the news."

"Did Axle tell you I saw a dead woman in a car on Clarkson Pass?"

Byron's grin fell off his face. "He mentioned it. Are you sure you saw—"

"Yes, yes," I interrupted him. Not Byron, too! I felt my eyebrows hovering near my hairline.

"I'm sorry ya had to see that, Delaney." The ear-splitting sound of a compressor filled the air. Byron indicated with a jerk of his head that we should remove ourselves to the quiet lobby.

I followed him inside, and when the door shut behind us, silence descended. I slouched into the fluffy brown sofa, and Byron perched on a stool in front of a computer and a cash register, hiking his heavy work boots onto the bottom rung. A warm mocha color covered the walls, green hanging plants lined up in front of the window, and car magazines overlapped neatly on the coffee table. A coffee machine with single-serve pods occupied a shelf in the corner. The lobby was cozy, and I suspected it was probably nicer now than when my dad ran the business.

"So, ya found another dead body?" The creases deepened in Byron's forehead.

I tightened my jacket around my chest. "No one seems to believe me, including you. Why won't you take my word for it? I've never exaggerated or told stories."

He was quick to assure me, "I believe you, I do…but

maybe it's one too many times. I mean, it's hard ta believe, ya know, in a way."

"It's not that uncommon to find dead people in cars. You know that, Byron." My voice had a little bit of a whine to it.

"I guess." He hunched forward resting his arms on his knees, and his eyes creased even deeper.

I decided not to mention the whiteboard I thought of as my "Murder Board." Byron was starting to look concerned. He'd never been married, as far as I knew, and didn't have any kids of his own, but he worried about me more than my own dad ever did. I shoved up from the couch and walked over to Byron, snaking my arm across his shoulder for a side-hug. "Don't stress out. It's all good."

He hung his head. "I cain't help worryin'. You get yerself in trouble all the time, Delaney. You know I care about you."

"I love you, too, Old Man, but there's no trouble, nothing I know about anyway." I gave him a tight squeeze, then let go. "I got a letter from Rob Abington."

"Why'd he write ta you?" He rocked back on his stool, and the seat groaned under his weight.

"Because I wrote to him. I asked him what he knew about Dad's death." The hit-and-run driver who forced my dad off the road had never been found.

"Why would he know anythin'?"

"He mentioned it a long time ago."

Byron's neck bent forward. "What'd his letter say?"

"Nothing, really. He didn't give me any answers." I blinked back annoying water in my eyes, and Byron pretended not to notice. What Rob had written was not helpful and felt like he was putting me off. "Hey, I have a tow to take care of. I need to get going." I fished in my purse for my keys.

"Be careful, Delaney," he said as I went out the door.

Spruce Ridge has three distinct sections. The ginormous mansions on the mountain side where the celebrities and millionaires lived, the historical and touristy district near Main Street where the working class lived, and a newer area with subdivisions, strip malls, and big box stores. That's where the coffee shop was and where I lived. The auto body shop was not far from Old Town.

After steering my tow truck down Main Street past trendy boutiques, breweries, and a coffee shop that rivaled Kristen's, I took another right and pulled to the curb in front of a white two-story with a wide front porch and black shutters. A Chrysler PT Cruiser with a front-wheel drive train and rusted side panels was parked in the driveway, nose-in to the garage door.

The three-inch heels of my trademark black stilettos hit the ground as I emerged from the truck cab, then the rest of me followed.

A man with lank hair and hollowed cheeks walked over. "Are you Del?"

"That's me." I liked it when my customers called me Del, my father's name. "You want the PT Cruiser transported across town?"

"I heard you're the tow truck driver who wears stilettos. I'd never have believed it if I hadn't seen it for myself."

I gave him a smile. "Well, now you've seen it. Where to?"

"L&B Garage."

I knew the place, not one of my favorites. Rob Abington had operated a chop shop at L&B. The cops shut down the illegal activity, Rob had gone to jail, and the legitimate side of the business managed to carry on. I told the customer the fee, and he paid by a credit card I swiped through my card reader.

"Can I watch?" he asked.

Normally I didn't mind showing off my skills, what little I had, but something seemed off about the guy. There was always a risk of running into trouble when working with the public like this.

"Not too close. Stand to the side, please. Over there, behind that tree." I pointed to a spot well away from me.

After he ambled off, I patted my pocket for the pepper spray—yes, it was there, and hopefully active—then I crouched down in my heels to release the tow dolly from the truck's undermount.

Here's the deal with towing—if a car is front-wheel drive, it has to be lifted from the front, if rear-wheel, it has to be lifted from the rear, and if all-wheel, all four tires have to be elevated. My Xtruder had an integrated wheel-lift system controlled hydraulically from inside the cab. The button on the wireless remote lowered the T-bar to the ground, the claws on the end of the boom grabbed one set of tires, either the front or the back, and the boom raised that end of the car. If I needed to lift both ends, I used tow dollies on the end not lifted by the boom.

In this case, the car was front-wheel drive, but since it was parked nose-in, my truck couldn't extract the vehicle from the front. I needed to tow from the rear, and that meant the front wheels had to be elevated with tow dollies. And my good buddy, Axle, had fabricated dolly undermounts so I didn't have to lift the heavy dollies down from the truck bed. I could roll them out on the ground, which I just did.

While wearing high heels.

And I'm such a professional for knowing all this.

A sudden stab of guilt hit my heart. All my expertise had been wasted when, instead of stopping, I sailed past that woman at the summit. I really hoped the road opened soon and that she would be found.

After securing the PT Cruiser's wheels with straps, I climbed inside my truck and waved to the customer. "You can come out from behind the tree now. Call your mechanic and let him know I'm on my way." He gave me a thumbs up, so I zoomed down the street, the PT Cruiser trundling along behind.

The guy had kept his distance after all. No need for the pepper spray. I'd only had to use it once before, and that wasn't on a hauling job. It was on a suspect while trying to solve a crime.

One of those previous homicides.

One of those situations Byron worried about.

And me, too.

Chapter 3

Ephraim walked through my apartment door just as the oven timer went off.

"Time to eat." I grinned.

"Hello to you, too." He hooked an arm around my neck and gave me a kiss.

He went for the silverware and napkins while I dished up the southwestern shepherd's pie, a mixture of hamburger, black beans, and cumin topped with mashed sweet potatoes. Normally at the sound of the timer, Axle showed up salivating like a rat in a cheese maze, but he was downstairs at the coffee shop practicing with the band. Boss drooled at my feet, though, so I spooned a couple of dollops into his food bowl on the floor.

I set two long-necked beers near our plates along with a basket of tortilla chips. "How was your day?"

"Fine. Not very exciting for a change."

"No women have gone missing?" I asked.

"What?" He'd just settled his napkin across his lap.

"You were going to check on missing women."

"Oh, that. None reported in the immediate area."

"Zach hasn't called to let me know whether the road is open." Boss nosed my foot under the table, and I passed him a chip.

"It's not, but if this clear weather holds, it shouldn't take too long."

"I'm glad." I hoped that poor woman would be found before too much longer. "Axle's band is playing downstairs tonight."

"You want to go later?"

"*Ab-so-freaking-lutely.*" I needed to support my l'il cuz, and the band was actually pretty good.

We finished most of the pie while discussing a movie we'd been wanting to see. Then I put the food away, Ephraim loaded the dishwasher, and we slumped together on one of the facing loveseats. Ephraim stretched out his legs and crossed his cowboy boots at the ankles. The word art on the wall above us spelled out "Family," and the mismatched sofa pillows shouted out shabby chic, the style I loved. Kristen had given me the plaque because she and I were like sisters. I'd always felt content here.

I cuddled against Ephraim, and he brushed a strand of hair back from my face. He tilted my head and found a soft spot on the side of my neck with his lips. A jolt of electricity ran down the length of my body.

"About missing women...did you check outside the immediate area?" I asked.

"Hundreds of thousands of people go missing in the United States each year." He spoke softly into my ear.

"No one seems worried about this woman. Not law enforcement. Not anybody, it seems."

He sighed. "Be patient. The pass will reopen. The area will be searched. Your little mystery solved."

"*My* little mystery. My *little* mystery?" I had my finger in his face.

"I didn't mean it like that."

"Humph." I knew exactly how he meant it. I drew my legs into my chest and wrapped my arms around my knees. A couple months ago I'd accused him of cheating. I was overreacting then; am I overreacting now? Am I being fair or am I blowing this out of proportion?

The sheriff had the reputation of being a player, a hot-blooded Latino pursuing not only a law enforcement career but all the single women in town, too. That was all in the past, he'd assured me. Even though I was wrong about him cheating, I'd always felt the cowboy-Casanova would leave me for another woman eventually. Probably, if I was honestly analyzing myself, those thoughts had something to do with my dad. He didn't keep in touch with me after the divorce.

Abandonment is my trigger. Am I worried Ephraim was going to ditch me—like my dad did? Maybe I'm looking for a reason to dump Ephraim first. Something I don't want to admit, even to myself. I pushed that fatherless little girl inside me to the back of my mind.

Ephraim's confused eyes studied me. "Dinner was great, like something my mom would make." He was trying to get on my good side now. His mama was a superb cook.

"Thanks. That's the best compliment." I unwrapped my knees and placed a hand against his cheek. He captured my fingers, landing a kiss on my palm. *Oooh*, that was nice. Okay, maybe this grudge I had against him was overplayed, and I needed to let go of my hard feelings.

He crushed his lips to mine and my pulse spiked, but I caught something out of the corner of my eye—Axle emerging from the hallway.

Ephraim and I jolted upright.

"I didn't know you were home, Axle. I thought you were downstairs with the band." My voice came out shrill.

"Just woke up." He yawned. His hair stuck up all over in a bed head, and he smoothed it down. "What smells so good?"

"Southwestern shepherd's pie. You hungry?" Silly question. Of course, he was. I got up off the couch to retrieve the casserole and made him a plate, channeling my mother. After he wolfed down a few bites, I said, "I'd thought you'd be getting ready for tonight, Ax."

He glanced at his phone. "Heading down now. You're coming, right?"

Ephraim said, "Wouldn't miss it."

When Axle hustled out the door, I put his plate in the dishwasher and the casserole back in the fridge. I grabbed my purse and keys and said to Ephraim, "We might as well head down now, too."

He nodded. "Let's go."

When we walked through the coffee shop's door, all the tables were taken. One corner was heavy with groups of teens. Kristen was busy at the pickup counter, two baristas took orders, and another barista made drinks. Ephraim got in line and I walked up to Kris. "Wow. An early crowd, huh?"

"Yes." Her face was pink with excitement. "One of the judges for the restaurant contest is here. Oliver Clang. Oliver runs the online newspaper in Spruce Ridge." She nodded toward a table in front of the stage where a man sat alone. He seemed to be in his forties, with a pinched expression and short strawberry-blond hair. He wore bright orange tennis shoes.

"He's hogging a table. I think I'll ask him if we can sit with him."

Kristen nodded and plucked a cup off the rack to fill

an order. While Ephraim waited for our drinks, I walked up to the contest judge. "Do you mind sharing a table?"

"Not at all." He got up to pull out an empty chair for me.

"Thanks." I sat down.

Mace, one of the members of the band, wound his way between the guitar stands and drums and strode over. His eyes were dark and broody, his hair shoulder-length, a stereotypical creative type. He said to Clang, "Justin wants to know, are you going to give us a write-up?" I remembered Justin was the name of the bass guitar player and in charge of promoting the band.

"Planning on it." Clang nodded. Mace motioned him closer, and they had a few quiet words to themselves while I tried to look elsewhere. Mace made his way back to the stage now complete with the other musicians and slung his guitar strap over his shoulder.

He gave *a one, a two, a three*, and the music began. Mace stood to the right of Kelsey, the lead singer and lone female, and Justin, the bass player, stood to her left. Directly behind Kelsey, Axle pounded the drums like a thumper on caffeine. When he returned to a *kick-snare-kick-snare* rhythm, Kelsey stepped up to the microphone.

Ephraim took the seat between Clang and me and set our espressos in front of us. All eyes were on Kelsey, so I sneaked a look at Ephraim. Ephraim was giving her an appreciative eye, and on the other side of the sheriff, Clang's gaze combed over the singer as well. Then his head whipped in my direction and he caught me staring at him.

I snapped my gaze to Kelsey who swayed with the music. Axle tossed one drumstick in the air, I held my breath, but he caught it, and I breathed a sigh of relief.

He stirred brushes on the snare drum while she reached some high notes.

I chanced another look at Clang. His face started to glisten with sweat and his hands white-knuckled his coffee cup, then he pushed back from the table and carried his cup to the counter. I couldn't help but stare at the orange sneakers that made him eligible for a fashion fine. I got one more glimpse of him before he disappeared out the door. I crossed my fingers and hoped the judge didn't have an upset stomach from too much caffeine. Would Kris lose points in the restaurant contest if he'd gotten sick?

When Kelsey finished the chorus and stepped back from the mic, all the men in the band displayed dimwitted looks that I'd call smitten, the poor guys. After the band played the instrumental ending, a lank-haired man gave the musicians thunderous applause and yelled out a couple of hurrahs. I remembered him; I'd just towed his PT Cruiser. He'd given me a bad vibe then, and my opinion didn't improve now. The man whistled and hooted, drawing more attention to himself, and I was embarrassed for him.

The band played for another hour. The last song wound down, and at the end of the show, the enthusiastic fan rushed over to the musicians. "Great job. Fantastic set. Can I help you with anything? Packing up? Anything?"

The men in the band looked to Kelsey who said, "Not tonight, Barlow. Thanks."

The man's face fell. Ephraim ushered him toward the door, and he shuffled out with the rest of the crowd.

The musicians unplugged their guitars and put them into cases. Ephraim flipped the Open sign to Closed, I swept and mopped the floor, and Kristen loaded the dishwasher and balanced the register. The baristas finished the end-of-service procedures and left. Ephraim took the garbage to the dumpster, and all of us separated in the parking lot, the sheriff and musicians for their cars, and Axle, Kristen, and I for our apartments upstairs.

I told Kristen on the landing between our doors, "That was a great time."

"Yeah. The proceeds made it worthwhile. Thanks, cousin." She threw her arms around Axle, but by his stiff stance it was obvious he didn't want the bear hug, and she let her arms drop. Smiling, she worked the key in her door and pushed it open. "See you in the morning," she said, vanishing inside.

I buddy-punched him in the arm. "You did good, Ax. Kristen is happy."

"*Whatevs*. Let's make sure Boss doesn't get out." He opened the apartment door, threw out his elbows, squatted down on his heels, and kicked his legs out like a Greek dancer hopping his way inside, which I admit was effective in keeping his dog from making a run for it. Once I shut the door, Axle jerked to a stand. "Want some ice cream?"

"No, thanks." I toed off my heels and they fell to the floor with a thunk. I left them there and shuffled over to the couch. My li'l cuz brought his dish of ice cream to the living room and sat down across from me.

"Everything going okay with you, Axle? You haven't come with me on tows lately."

"Yeah, the band's been taking up all my time." He shot me a sideways look, spoon halfway to his mouth. "You managing on your own?"

"Sure." But I missed him. Instead of chatting with

Axle while waiting on calls for tows, I'd taken to playing solitaire on my phone, but that was not as good a companion as Axle. Hard to admit to myself, but true. "You had some fans tonight. There was one guy I thought was going to fling a bearing. Kelsey called him Barlow. He was—"

He held up his spoon to cut me off. "Barlow Harmen. He is too much. We can't get rid of the guy."

I scrunched up my nose. "A stalker fan?"

"Yup, he's a STAN all right."

"Well, think of it this way. Your first STAN."

Axle made a derisive noise, put his bowl in the sink, and we headed to our separate rooms. I gave an involuntary shudder. A stalker fan was the price of success. Made me glad I was a simple car hauler.

****

The next morning another weather alert indicated snow was hitting the mountains again. Smoky white clouds obscured the peaks in the distance, and I knew there was bound to be icy conditions at higher elevations. The body was not going to be found yet. No way Clarkson Pass would open today.

And no way I'd wear heels today.

It was a snow boots kind of a day, even if the bad weather didn't stretch as far down the pass as Spruce Ridge.

After dropping off Axle at Oberly Motors and retrieving my truck, I entered the westbound lane of I-70 to look for orange-tagged stalls ticketed by the police for removal. The snow was scraped down to the pavement and piled up on the side of the road, but the highway surface was wet with icy patches just as I'd expected. Flocks of brown geese dotted the snow-covered fields on either side of the road and traffic was light. I drove to the exit for County Road 350, checked that the gate up to the pass was closed, then returned to the highway. I came across an occupied Lexus RX 350—that's a front-wheel drive, high-end SUV—against the metal barrier separating westbound traffic from the forest of close-growing pines.

I weaseled my truck into the narrow space and threw the gear into park. Snow immediately collected on my windshield and I flipped on the light bar. I shimmied out of the cab to avoid any oncoming traffic and edged over to the Lexus driver's door, my boots kicking up snow with each step.

I motioned the man inside to roll down his window. "Are you all right?"

"I slid off the road and hit the guardrail."

"I'll be right back." I skirted around the front end and peered between the passenger's side and the concrete barrier. The side panel was deeply dented and black marks scraped the concrete block. I noticed some damage to the front end, too, but the wheels were in good shape.

I said when I returned, "Why don't you get in my cab, and I'll hook you up." He inched open his door, but I had second thoughts. Before he could get out completely, I asked, "Was there another car involved?" He shook his head side to side. "You have insurance to cover this?"

"What, are you a cop?"

"No, but I work with the police."

He shoved the door all the way open, knocking me into the traffic lane. I stumbled back, stunned, while he took off running down the icy shoulder, his oversized hiking boots making quick traction. A horn blasted, a car swerved around me, and I quick-stepped out of the way. People don't move over for tow trucks like they should.

"Hey, get back here," I yelled, but the man kept going. It wasn't my job to chase after him, but I wondered if the Lexus was stolen. That might cause someone to run, so I called 9-1-1. The VIN was visible through the windshield and I provided the numbers to the dispatcher.

Waiting in my cab, I opened a game of free solitaire and played a few hands. I'd put the eight on the nine and the ten on the jack when a Spruce Ridge cruiser showed up and Zach climbed out.

"I called it in right away this time." I waited for him to acknowledge my good deed, but he didn't, so I pointed out, "The driver ran off when I questioned him."

"I checked the VIN you provided, and the car's not stolen."

"Oh?" I experienced a pang of disappointment.

"Could be the driver was wanted for something, though."

I perked up. "I can look through mug shots."

"Are you kidding? We make twenty thousand arrests a year in this county alone."

"That many?" Jeez, what's up with that? "So, do you want me to move the Lexus off the highway?"

"Yes." He shaded his eyes with one hand over his brow and looked in the distance. "The guy's probably long gone, but I'll drive around and keep an eye out for him." He turned back to me. "Delaney, I came up here because you called, but an abandoned car is not an emergency. Next time, just report it to the desk, and it will get orange tagged."

"Okay, Zach."

"So, don't call 9-1-1 again."

"Got it." I waved my hand in dismissal. "Enough said." I let him pull out before I climbed in the truck cab to hitch the Lexus to the boom. I'd done my duty, even if Zach thought my call wasn't worth his time. I can't seem to get anything right lately.

Once I had the Lexus in tow, the thought hit me. Did the driver run because he'd killed that poor woman on the pass? Something no one else seemed to be paying any mind to…there could be a killer on the loose. If only people believed me. If only I hadn't been alone. If Axle had been with me—or if I'd been able to afford to hire help—I would've had someone in the truck with me, a witness to what I'd seen on the pass. Zach and everyone else would've believed me then. Oh well, what did I care? I believed in myself and that was enough.

****

When I walked in the door of our apartment, Axle and Boss faced me like a welcoming committee, but they both wore guilty looks. Boss slunk over to me and his cold wet nose poked my hand. Axle said, "Don't get mad, Delaney."

"I hate it when someone tells me that." I looked past Axle to pieces of white Styrofoam all over the floor.

"Boss chewed on your whiteboard." He gave me an apologetic look.

"Shame on you," I scolded Boss with my hands on my hips.

"You know what else? He ran outside and got halfway to the parking lot before I caught him."

I told the *Rottie* in a stern voice, "You need to behave, Boss," and then said to Axle, "Something's wrong here. Why's he been trying to escape lately?"

Ax raised his shoulders and let them fall.

Aware Axle and I were talking like the parents of a wayward teen, I scrunched the dog's ears until he leaned in to me.

Axle pointed toward my bedroom. "Go see the damage."

I walked the length of the hall with Axle and the *Rottie* on my heels. Only one corner of the board was missing, although Boss had managed to make a chewed-up mess on the floor.

"You know what this is?" I asked Axle.

"It's written across the top. Murder Board. A dead giveaway." He laughed. "Did you catch that? Dead?" He laughed again and flipped my braid which flew up and hit me in the face.

"Hey." I smoothed my plait down. "Real mature."

"So, you think it's murder then?"

"I don't know, but yes, I think it might be." I lifted the board and carried it out to the living room, propping it on the couch, where Boss promptly jumped up and sank his teeth into it.

"Oh, come on!" I yelled, and he scrambled down, tail between his legs. "He obviously likes to chew on this so I'm taking it downstairs."

"The band's about ready to practice, so I'm coming, too."

We descended the outside staircase. A new barista stood behind the cash register, and I gave my usual order, a double espresso. No other customers waited in line, and the dining area was empty except for the band and that creepy Barlow, the STAN, or stalker fan.

Kris came out of her office. "What've you got

there?"

I held it up for her to see and tapped the heading. "Murder Board. You know, the dead woman I saw. Remember?"

Kris nodded and studied the board. She always believed in me, even when I doubted myself. The musicians and lone fan gathered round, squinting at the vague hand-drawn map, the stick figure, and the cartoonish drawing of the car.

Mace tossed back his long hair. "Why do you think it's murder? How did she die?" His last name was Mason. I don't know his first name, but everyone called him Mace.

"I have no idea." I pointed to that same question I'd written on the board. "Do you guys have any suggestions? Nothing obvious, like a gunshot wound. I think I would've seen that."

Axle snorted and I gave him my super-laser glare. A *whoa* expression appeared on his face, but he said, "Maybe it's not murder. It could be something else. I know, she was kicked by a horse."

"Maybe she drowned?" This was Justin.

Everyone laughed. It wasn't surprising that Axle was making fun of me, but the others were taking his lead now.

"How about hit by a falling coconut? Hey, I heard that's a real thing," Mace said.

Barlow asked, "Was there a noose around her neck?" I'm afraid I gave him a sharp look since he seemed more gruesome than the others.

"Very funny. Quit teasing. I'm serious here." I looked from one to the other.

Kelsey scrunched her brow in concentration. "She

was waiting for her lover and froze to death."

All the guys gazed at her in awe. Axle said, "That's really good, Kels. You're right, that's what happened." They nodded as if she were an oracle. The musicians didn't take me seriously, but now that Kelsey said it, they believed her?

I turned from the men to focus on the woman. The first time I'd met her was last night at the band's performance, but Axle had already told me a lot about her and that she had a good voice. She was tall and slender, with dyed black hair, black nail polish, and a cute, pouty face. There was something familiar about her. She reminded me of someone I'd seen before. Kelsey would warrant close to a ten on a scale of ten, and the guys? Well, maybe a four. Just being honest.

Axle bumped shoulders with Kelsey. "You're brilliant." She mock punched him back.

The muscles bunched in my throat. It was usually Axle and me who regressed into pushing and shoving. I wasn't jealous—Axle was ten years younger than me—but it felt like I was losing a friend. Some friends stay forever, like Kristen, and some friends didn't last, but I thought Axle was the staying, lasting kind.

Kelsey turned to me with a sad face. "So, is there really a dead body up there on the pass?"

We all seemed to sense a presence behind us and spun around at the same time.

Kris stammered out, "Why, it's Mr. Rizzo." How long had he been standing there? She blushed under his gaze, then explained to the rest of us, "This is one of the judges in the restaurant contest." The man was dressed in a suit with highly polished shoes, a much different appearance than the judge with the bright orange sneakers who was here last night.

The musicians hoofed it back to their instruments, and Barlow followed them, leaving Kris and me with the newcomer.

Kristen asked him, "What can I do—" but the band struck up a loud tune and extinguished her words. Axle pounded the bass drum, *bam-bam-bam-badump-bump*. The musicians bounced their heads to the beat, their hair flying.

"What?" Mr. Rizzo hollered.

"Can I help you—" Kris started to say. *Bam-bam-bam-bam* went the drums. She stormed over to Axle. "Stop!" Her hands were over her ears. "Quit that." She motioned for the band to lower the decibels.

The music stopped on discordant notes, but when Kris turned back to the judge, he flung out his arms and said, "Now is obviously not a good time," then shot out the door. Kristen looked distraught as she watched him take off.

I stuck my Murder Board in Kris's office where Boss couldn't get to it, the written side hidden against the wall, and came back out to the front to order a caramel macchiato to go.

As Kristen handed me the drink, she asked, "Do you think that judge is going to ding me?" Kris was hoping for the grand prize of ten thousand dollars to invest back into her business. Ten thousand dollars, a nice certificate to frame on the wall, and a write-up in the local newspaper.

I forced a smile. "No way."

It was a complete lie, and she knew it. It was possible he'd heard our whole conversation. Between morbid jokes on horrible ways to die and the ear-splitting music, she'd probably lost plenty.

Chapter 4

The stretch of road leading to the Abington Auto Store was busy with the usual traffic. I left my self-loader around back near the oil-changing bay and entered through the front door. The receptionist knew me and waved me through to the manager's office where I found Nancy Abington who'd taken over the car dealership after her husband, Rob, went to jail and she'd divorced him.

"Delaney, you brought me a coffee." She extended her ring-covered fingers, and I stretched across her glass desk to hand her the cup. Her precision hairstyle and classy tailored suit looked expensive. "For what do I owe the pleasure?"

"Couple of things." I took the chair across from her. "Do you have any repos for me?"

"If I did I'd have someone call you."

"Thanks. I appreciate you, Nancy."

She gave me repo assignments from time to time, which helped supplement my income. A successful business owner, she was a good mentor to me and one of the restaurant contest judges. And better yet, she knew my mom. That would be a good card to play.

"So, my mom says to tell you hello." I wasn't lying. Mom always said that.

"Tell Eve hello back from me and I'll call her for

lunch soon."

"I will." I looked down in my lap and felt Nancy's gaze.

She asked, "What are you really here for?"

I considered the woman in front of me. There were so many things she could help me with, but I chose the most important one first. "Kristen over at Roasters on the Ridge entered the Top Ranked Restaurant contest in the coffee shop category, and I know you're one of the judges. I was hoping you could tell me how she's doing. She thought she was getting top marks, but she's not sure anymore. Mr. Rizzo came by last night but he left in a hurry." First, Clang of the orange sneakers, then Rizzo of the polished wingbacks, seemed to have fled from Roasters on the Ridge. Neither was a good sign.

"Delaney, I can't comment on any of the contestants. But I will say this, Nic Rizzo is with the Health & Safety Department, and since Roasters always gets top ratings from Health & Safety, that will go a long way with him. And you know I like Kristen." She held up her coffee and waggled the cup back and forth.

"She does have the best coffee in town." I couldn't help but tack that on.

"And you can bring me one of these any time." She gave me a broad smile. "You know there's also a fourth judge, a mystery judge?"

A fourth? In addition to Nancy Abington, Oliver Clang, and Nic Rizzo?

I shook my head.

"Even I don't know who that person is. The mystery judge shows up incognito and makes an evaluation based on how the average customer is treated."

"It's a good thing Kristen treats all her customers the

same. Everyone is special to her."

"You're so right. I'll give you a call if we need a vehicle recovered."

"Thanks, Nancy." I rose from my chair. "There is something else." Suddenly my mouth turned as dry as dusty pine needles, and I had to force out the words, "Umm, I wrote Rob at the prison."

The corners of her mouth twitched down. "You mentioned some time ago that you might. Did you hear back from him?"

"I did." The unhelpful words in his letter filtered through my mind. "He said to ask *you* about my dad's death."

"*Me?* I don't know why he would say that." She tilted her head quizzically as if she was thinking for a moment. "I'm sorry I can't help you. I know you want answers, but I don't have them."

"All right." I sighed a little too noisily. Was Rob just avoiding my questions by leading me on a goose chase?

"Maybe you misunderstood him." She crossed her arms and looked past me out the window.

I think I just offended her. I couldn't fault her for it, as if I'd taken Rob's side or something. No one should take sides in a divorce. But vague though they were, her former husband's words were hard to misunderstand: *To answer your question, who caused your dad's death, ask my wife.*

But I said, "Sorry, Nancy, maybe I did. I think Rob's trying to put me off."

No one had been convicted or arrested for causing my dad's fatal hit and run. The other driver was never identified. But before he was incarcerated, Rob hinted to me that he knew something about Dad's accident. I suspected Rob not only had information, but that he was involved somehow, although I wasn't hopeful for a confession. Rob had been convicted for grand theft auto and running a chop shop, but one of his employees was also found guilty for the murder of an innocent man (not my dad), which he claimed was on Rob's orders. That claim was never proven. It was unlikely Rob would admit anything to me in writing, especially since outgoing prison mail was monitored. And if Nancy truly didn't know—I suppose I had no reason to doubt her—then Rob was only trying to deflect blame and make trouble for his ex-wife. And I was causing that trouble.

But what if Rob had told the truth? What if Nancy was hiding information that could blow my dad's investigation wide open? I thought Nancy and I were friends, and I would expect a friend to tell me. Since she didn't, I had to trust this lead was a dead end.

"Well, I'll get going. I'll let you get back to your business, Nancy."

Her face had a pinched look, so I left her office and made tracks for my truck.

I phoned Mom from the driver's seat, put the call on speaker, and cranked the engine. When she picked up, I said, "I just saw Nancy Abington. She's going to call you for lunch."

"That'd be great." Mom was thrilled. She liked to feel in the center of things. She went on to tell me her news about the neighbors I hardly knew and her husband, Will's, law partners, who I didn't know at all, but that was Mom for you. "Anything new with you?" she finally asked.

"Kristen entered the Top Ranked Restaurant contest and Nancy's one of the judges."

"I'll put in a good word, but Kristen will win anyway, I have no doubt." Mom totally got it. Kris was like Mom's second daughter because Kris and I had been friends since elementary school. We'd remained close. When Kris opened her coffee shop in Spruce Ridge, she'd asked me to help, and I jumped at the chance. I'd only recently made the career change from barista to full-time tow truck driver.

I said, "Okay, good. I think I may have offended Nancy, so I'd appreciate help in smoothing things over with her."

"What in the world did you say?"

"I asked her about Rob."

"Oh, that explains it. No woman likes to talk about her ex. She'll get it over it."

"Thanks, Mom." I hoped she was right. I didn't bother to mention that I'd brought up Mom's ex, my dad, with Nancy.

Avoidance, much?

After we disconnected, I turned the truck toward my apartment and arrived home within minutes. My footsteps echoed on the stairs as I made my way to the door. Axle was in the kitchen spreading peanut butter on a slice of bread, and Boss begged at his feet.

"Hey, Ax. You home for lunch?"

"How'd you figure that one out?"

"I'm smart like that." I pried open the refrigerator and peered inside. Two hard-boiled eggs. Good enough. I started cracking the shells on a paper towel. "Axle, why does the band have to practice at Roasters?"

His gray eyes so like Kristen's flicked up at me. "Kris said we could."

"Of course she did."

He squared his normally slouched shoulders. "What's the beef?"

"Have you checked out other places?"

"No, her place is so convenient. We can dock our instruments there, and I don't have to leave the drums across town. Why? Did she say anything to you?"

"Kris didn't say anything, but the band is costing her points in the competition. When that judge, Rizzo, came by Roasters to talk to Kris, your music drove him off."

"No, Delaney, you're the one costing her points."

I gave him a hard jab to the bicep. "No, you're the one."

"No, you." He rubbed his arm where I'd poked him, but he didn't punch me back like he usually did. His Rottweiler woofed and crouched in a play bow, thinking he was going to join the fun. Axle put the peanut butter away. "Delaney, dead up, for real. When the judge heard you talking about murder, well, that was *très* lame."

I gave a little sigh. So, okay, the little twerp wasn't wrong.

He said, "Justin needs a place to crash tonight. I told him he can take the couch."

"All right. Thanks for letting me know." I slid my eggs into a plastic baggy and tucked it in my purse to eat on the road. Then I leaned my hip against the counter. "Tell me about the members of the band, Axle. How do you know them?"

"Justin and me, we were in high school band together. Justin knows Kelsey from college. He's a cinematography major and I think Kelsey's in performing arts or something. And Mace, let's see—him and me worked together at L&B Garage."

"You were in high school band? You were a band

nerd?"

"What did you think I was? A stoner?"

"I never." I totally did.

"I wasn't a nerd. I played the drums. Chicks dig it."

Laughter burst out of me.

His eyes pinched into sharp arrows. "What? I'm not cool? That coming from you?"

"Sorry. Band must've gotten cooler after I left high school."

"That was before time began."

I felt taken down a notch. "Good one. So, you know Mace from L&B Garage? Does he still work there?"

"Nah, he was a ski instructor over the winter. I think he's between jobs now. Except for gigs, of course."

"Huh. So, how likely is it for you to meet another musician working as a mechanic like yourself?"

"A lot of people play guitar. What's a gift from the universe is Kelsey. It's a miracle we met up with her. She can sing like a rock star." He smiled when he said her name. The poor guy had a crush.

"Did Mace know L&B was a chop shop?" The garage had been shut down, and how it managed to reopen as a legitimate car repair business was beyond me.

"You'll have to ask him." His fingers beat an imaginary drum solo in the air. "Kelsey heard from somebody that a music scout is going to stop by and watch the band perform. We're all jazzed about it."

"That's amazing, Axle." I nodded, pleased for my li'l cuz. "I'm looking for stalls this afternoon. You want to ride along and tell me about it?"

"No. I have an errand to run. Then practice. I need to get going." Axle bit into his sandwich and headed for the door.

"I'm leaving, too." I locked the door after us and clattered down the steps behind him. He finished his sandwich by the time he jumped into his Nissan Altima, front-wheel drive. I pulled myself up into my truck cab, and together we took off down Pine Street. His Altima was fully operational today, if you can believe that. It's normally in pieces at Oberly Motors, but he must've put it back together.

Axle went through the yellow at the intersection and I stopped for the light. Even though it was a cool day in April, runners in jogging gear, moms pushing strollers, and teens chatting together cleared the crosswalk. A man and a woman cycled toward the river trail. Everyone in Spruce Ridge lived outside as much as possible, weather permitting. And why not? The majesty of the mountains was right outside our front doors. And it was spring. The mountain peaks were still getting snow, but the flowering trees were about to pop everywhere else.

Lately Axle had been too busy to go with me on tows. We had fun with the insults and banter—I exist to aggravate Axle—but the band seemed to occupy all his spare time, and he didn't hang with me as much. Maybe he and I were in different places and the age gap was causing the wedge. Axle was only out of high school by a year and most of his friends were college age including his girlfriend, Shannon, who was at university. I'd graduated from college over five years ago with a degree I didn't use. I always felt that Axle was like family, but now I felt he was growing away from me.

I spent the rest of the afternoon trolling for vehicles on the side of the road, orange-tagged by the city for removal, didn't find any, and arrived at the towaway zones at five o'clock. Thursday nights were usually busy with everyone at the breweries starting the weekend early. The alley behind Main Street was a convenient place to snug away a car and avoid paying a parking meter, but I was hired to haul away the cars that blocked the loading docks.

I sat in the alley idling the engine. Traffic hummed on Main Street, but the alley remained deserted, so I checked the CDOT website for road conditions—the pass was still closed—and played about a hundred games of free solitaire.

At eight o'clock, I bobbed my shoulders up and down in a stretch and craned my neck around. Farther down the alley I spotted a Mercury Milan, front-wheel drive, illegally parked in front of the art studio's loading dock. The Milan was reversed into the parking spot with its front end fully accessible. I backed my truck to its bumper and hit the button on the remote to lower the T-bar. The scoops captured the tires, the boom lifted the Milan, and I pulled forward. My self-loader was amazing, and I always got a lot of satisfaction from the truck's performance.

Before I could turn out of the alley, a teenager in a ballcap waved me down. I opened my window. "Is this your car?"

"Yeah. Do you have to tow it? Can I have it back?"

"You did see the towaway warning sign, right?"

"What sign?" He feigned innocence.

"Really? That's what you're going with?"

"Okay, I saw the sign."

"I could charge you a drop fee, but I won't this time. Stand back." I retrieved the remote from under the dash. With a groan and a whiff of hydraulic fluid, the boom lowered the vehicle, the front tires hit the ground with a soft *pumpf*, the claws retracted, and the crossbar folded onto the truck bed with a final squeak.

The kid jumped into his Milan and reversed all the way down the alley, kicking up slush as it went.

****

That night I dreamt I was walking along a wooded path holding a flashlight. The light illuminated a woman. She faced me. Her skin was white, her mouth pouty, and her eyes out of focus. Suddenly it was Kelsey's face and I woke up. I shook my head. Where had that awful dream come from? I assured myself it was because I'd gotten a good look at Kelsey, really looking at her for the first time, just the other day. That's all it was.

Snoring bombarded my ears from the direction of the living room. I lurched out of bed and tugged strands of hair out of my mouth before working my way down the hall. Justin was sprawled on one of the loveseats, a sofa pillow under his head, mouth open, with whistling sounds coming from his nose. Mace was on the floor in a sleeping bag, and Kelsey was under an afghan on the other loveseat. The whole band was here.

Axle had only told me about Justin. It was all I could do not to wake Axle up and give him a whack on the head. Don't think I didn't consider it.

A loud rumble like the sound of a rockslide came from the sleeping bag. So Mace was the guilty one. I'd never be able to sleep with the thundering *zzzzKKKKKzzzzzKKKKKznork!*

With my blanket, pillow, and laptop for good measure, I picked my way past the slumberers, went out the door with everything, including my keys, and let myself in the back door of the coffee shop. I made up a bed in one of the booths and turned on the white noise app on my computer, but it didn't blot out the noises keeping me awake, the occasional sounds of traffic and whirring appliances that couldn't be heard during the day.

I turned off the white noise and went to the search engine to query women missing in Clear Creek County. Ephraim was correct that there were no recent reports, and there were too many irrelevant hits to provide any real information. All this data was exhausting, so I tried to sleep again but couldn't. I checked the weather forecast and played a few card games before my eyes drooped.

A knock on the window made me sit up. I twirled around to see a man looking through the glass with a raised-eyebrow grimace, and I sucked in a scream, my pulse taking off like a race car at the starting gate.

I looked closer. It was only Nic Rizzo. One of the restaurant contest judges.

He puffed out his cheeks and mouthed, "Open the door," then walked toward the entryway and beckoned me over.

I took a deep breath, rubbed my sleepy eyes, and went to turn the lock. "Yes, Mr. Rizzo? Can I help you with something?"

He stepped across the threshold, his frame filling the doorway. His dark hair was slicked back, and he wore a trench coat and dress pants with his polished wingback shoes. So formal for the middle of the night. "Are you sleeping in the coffee shop?" he asked.

That popped my eyes open. Where was he going with this? How should I answer? If I said yes, was that a Health Code violation? If I said no, would that bring up another infraction?

"Is there anything wrong?"

"There could very well be. What are you doing here after hours?" He waved his hands around in wide gestures.

My words tumbled out fast. "I couldn't sleep so I came down here. Kristen and I live in the apartments over the shop." I stabbed my upraised finger toward the ceiling. "I was playing solitaire on my computer. Not sleeping." I showed him my laptop with cards bouncing all over the screen.

"It's two in the morning. You aren't sleeping here?"

"You'd think so, but no." I looked down at my pajama top that read, "Don't bother me, I'm sleeping." I asked, "You aren't going to take points away from Kristen, are you?"

He shrugged a who-knows gesture, his palms up, fingers waving in my face. "It's unlawful for a person to sleep in any bakeshop, kitchen, dining room, or other place where food is served."

Uh-oh, not good.

"I wasn't, I swear. And I'm leaving right now." I grabbed the pillow and blanket. "See, I'm outta here."

He aimed a hard look at me. "Good."

He stepped outside and I followed in his wake, locking the door after us. I jogged around the side of the building to head for the rear stairs, and I cast a last glance back to find him watching me. I gave him a thumbs up and called out, "Good night, sleep tight."

Jeez, why'd I say that? Mental kick in the butt.

Once back in bed, I wondered what the restaurant judge was doing here at this time of night. Was he checking the contestants during the wee hours? Why? Or was he out for another reason? It didn't really matter to me if he was, but still, I was curious. Then I asked myself, would he really take points away from Kristen, and worse, would she find out?

Yes and yes.

Yeah, it blows.

I punched my pillow a couple of times, resigned to a noisy, sleepless night.

Chapter 5

I'd just poured my morning coffee when I saw Mom's number light up my screen. Her voice was shrill over the line, "You found a dead body?"

"What are you talking about?"

"It was on the radio this morning. Something about how a tow truck operator spotted a dead woman trapped in the avalanche on Clarkson Pass. The Department of Transportation has been on double-time trying to clear the snow."

My eyebrows bumped up an inch. "How'd you know that was me?"

"They didn't mention you by name, but they didn't need to. The high-heeled tow truck driver from Spruce Ridge. Everyone knows that's you. The news even knocked all the recent bear sightings out of the headlines."

I rubbed one eye with the heel of my hand. "I did report a body in a parked vehicle, Mom. If you have to blame anyone, blame the highway patrol for sending me up the pass."

"Why didn't you tell me about this before now?"

"Well, I…um…" Eek. Caught. Guilty. Trying for a diversion, I said, "I wonder how the story about me got on the news."

"Police reports are generally public record. I know

that from Will." Mom's second husband Will was an attorney and someone I myself had called many times for information from public records.

"What radio station were you listening to? I want to see if I can catch the broadcast."

"You don't want to do that, Laney," she hedged, her voice low and worried.

Instant alert!

"Mom, tell me the station." I used my stern voice. She caved right away and handed over the call letters.

I crept past Axle's friends who were crashed in my living room and tiptoed back to my bedroom. I found the station and listened to the short reel that gave credit to an online news source, which I tracked down next. I had to scroll past an opinion piece that chemtrails from airplanes caused colin spasms to where I found the article that a female tow truck driver, famous for wearing high heels--*Famous?*--had left a car behind when she was supposed to evacuate the road. The writer suggested that I didn't want to get out of my truck and ruin my shoes. He went so far as to ask, "Did she see a dead body or not?"

It wasn't pretty.

These insults felt personal. I tried not to blow up, but sat on the bed fuming, mostly at myself. If I had gone back one more time to look, maybe I would have been able to locate the car. I wished I'd stopped one more time on the way down to check cell service. Maybe I could've alerted the police sooner. But would it have changed anything if she was already dead? And why didn't anyone believe me other than Kristen? Even Axle made fun of me.

Once the avalanche was cleared, the body would be

found and folks would be convinced then. I'd be sure to give Axle a hard time. He'd have to endure my I-told-you-so. Him and everyone else.

But why should I even care? I mean, caring too much about what others think only led to people-pleasing and a chance of losing myself.

Not going to happen. I'm living my true self, here.

And if foul play was involved, like I suspected, then I had my Murder Board ready. Don't forget, there could be a killer out there who thought he'd gotten away with murder.

I *will not* be mocked. (I imagined myself smacking Axle with his beanie.)

I *will* prove I'm right and uncover the killer. (If there was a murder.)

Been there, done that. (It's what I do.)

I may not be the best tow truck driver in town, but I wasn't too bad at digging around for clues.

I closed the news site, checked the road conditions—pass still closed—and put away my phone. After wriggling into my favorite sweater and jeans, I spent extra time on my makeup and hair—a smokey-eyed look and an oversized messy bun instead of a braid. I could at least appear to be someone sophisticated, someone who has it all together, someone credible who drew respect. My voice within scoffed at this, but I disregarded it.

The members of the band were gone when I came out. Axle was probably still sleeping in his room, so I trudged down the stairs to Roasters. Kristen would cheer me up. She was my calm and serene, yet fierce, friend who would put this all in perspective, and sure enough, entering her shop immediately plunged me into the comforting scent of coffee.

Nancy Abington waited at the pickup counter, thumbing her phone. "Good morning." I greeted her with a smile.

She looked up. "I heard that news about you on the radio."

"Oh?" I wrinkled my nose.

"That radio announcer was harsh." She tucked her phone back into her purse. "Everyone's asking if you really found another dead body."

I stuck out my chest. "Yes, Nancy, I did." Shaking her head, she gripped my shoulder for a moment then set off toward the tables.

As I headed to the backroom, Guy came around from behind the counter to stop me. "Delaney, this is so bad. Such a train wreck."

"So you heard the news, too?" The radio station was one everyone listened to.

"It's all over the place. I'm not sure how we're going to fix it. Kristen's in the office on the phone with a clean-up company now."

A clean-up company? What exactly was that? A public relations specialist? A social media expert? "Wow, Kris is the ultimate problem solver. I'm going back there." I skirted the counter and made my way at a speedy clip through the small kitchen with nothing more than a sink and dishwasher. I poked my head into Kristen's office.

She'd just hung up the phone. "You saw?"

"Well, I heard."

"Come outside with me." She exited the kitchen in three quick strides, and I practically stepped on her heels I was following so closely behind. When she went out the front door and twirled around to face the shop, I did the same, then stumble-halted with my mouth hanging open.

She linked her arm in mine. "It's not your fault."

Tears pricked my eyes. I opened my mouth, but words wouldn't come.

"The power sprayers are on their way here now. This will all be gone in an hour."

On the front of the building facing the street were the giant words, "Dead bodies everywhere," "I see dead people," and "Stilettos kick ass," and what looked like a colossal blood splatter. I had entered from the back and never saw it.

I slid from her grasp and ran my hands over the paint. "How easy will it be to get off?"

"The power washers told me they can remove it."

"Can we hose it off ourselves?"

"It'll be better to have the professionals do it. No one will even know it was here, Delaney." A kind smile creased her face, but the corner of Pine Street and Eagle Avenue was a busy intersection and even now traffic was jammed with drivers gawking at the spectacle. Everyone in this small town had most likely seen it already.

"This is all my fault. This is on me. Let me pay for the clean-up."

"No, stop." Kristen yanked on my arm. "No way. My insurance covers it."

Axle appeared on the sidewalk in his baggy jeans and hoodie that looked slept in. Squinting, he held a hand up to shade his eyes while he took in the damage. "This is the bomb."

"I thought you were still in bed," I said.

"Hey, what do you know?" He shrugged.

Why did this have to happen to Kristen? Really…if anyone wanted to make fun of me, they could have vandalized my Fiat…or my Fulcan Xtruder—gasp at the thought. Anything would have been better than defacing Roasters, my happy place and Kristen's livelihood. Wasn't that horrible news article enough? And the radio broadcast on top of that? What's going to happen next? Negative reviews? Boycotting my business? Or Kristen's?

"Delaney?" Axle nudged me. "Kris is talking."

"What?" I'd been so caught up in worry that I'd lost track of the conversation.

"The building will be freshly cleaned and all spruced up. It will look so nice." Kristen was obviously trying to focus on the bright side.

"Aren't you mad?" I asked her.

Axle said, "She never gets mad."

"I've seen her mad." I turned to Kris. "Remember when you cut the hair on your doll and it turned out really ugly and you threw the doll across the room?"

Kris rolled her eyes. "I was about eight."

"Then you stomped up and down and yelled. And the head popped off?"

"I said I was eight."

"Then you threw the head into the toilet and broke it and your parents had to call a plumber?"

Axle said, leaping in, "She said she was eight."

"Let's see. What about that time in college you had to read Plato for class, and you hated the book and tore it up and tried to flush the pages down the toilet?"

Axle shook his head. "A toilet again?"

"That was you, Delaney." Kristen laughed.

I drummed my fingers on my lips. "Oh yeah, that

was me."

Axle said, "See, I'm right. Kristen never loses it."

A truck, with Power Wash Perfect emblazoned on the door and a huge water tank strapped to the truck bed, pulled into the lot. A man got out and came toward us. When he reached us, he took Kris aside. She signed some paperwork and he headed back to his truck. Two other men climbed out and the three of them dragged hoses over to the building.

Kris, Ax, and I trooped back inside just as Nancy shouldered her way past us. She gave me a frown that seemed to be disapproving before she disappeared into the parking lot. I'm not sure what that was all about, but I didn't have time to think about it because my eye was caught by an empty award plaque hanging in the entryway, something I hadn't noticed before.

I asked Kris, "What's this? It's new."

Her face brightened. "That's for when I win the award for Top Ranked Restaurant in the coffee shop category."

"Nice." My throat constricted a tiny bit. How could she win with me around? I was left with a sick feeling in my stomach.

Just then Zach ripped open the door, and we jumped out of his way. "You all right, Kris?" he asked.

She smiled. "Of course."

He stuck out his hand. "Here's the incident report for your insurance claim."

She took hold of it. "Thanks. Come on back." She ushered him in the direction of her office.

I asked Axle, "You driving your Altima today or do you need a lift?"

"I'll catch a ride with you. Let's book it out of here."

After we grabbed coffees, with an extra one for the old man, we climbed into my Fiat and drove out of the parking lot. I signaled to turn off Pine onto Fifth and drove with zinging tires to Oberly Motors. Axle hopped out and darted into the auto bay. I opened the gate to retrieve my truck, and when I got out of the cab to lock the gate behind me, Byron came bustling out of the front entrance.

I reached inside for his to-go cup and handed it to him. "I was just about to bring this in for you. So, you and Axle pretty busy?"

"Yup, got a rush job ta do. And thanks for the coffee." He lifted the cup in the air. "Yer sweet to think o' me, Delaney. Yer such a good, kind person. And you look pretty today."

His compliments caused sudden tears to burn behind my eyes. He must have read the emotion on my face because he put an arm around my shoulders. "Now, now, what's the matter?"

"There's a story on the internet about me sighting the dead body and they made fun of me. And Kristen's coffee shop was tagged this morning. It's humiliating." I blinked away the unwanted tears.

"Come 'ere, you. I believe ya, and don't you go worryin' about what other people say." He held me tighter and patted my back like I was a child.

"I don't care about that, but what if I cost Kristen the competition?" I wiped my nose on the back of my hand.

"Ya won't. You an' everybody else are takin' this competition way too serious. It won't matter in another year or two."

"Right now it matters to Kristen. She's really hoping to win the prize money. She's thinking of all kinds of ways to invest it in her business. She's got a plaque all lined up on the wall to display the award certificate."

"Everyone already knows Roasters is the best coffee shop in town. She don't need an award certificate to tell 'er that." Byron tapped a finger on the hood of my truck. "Ya have to wonder, though, why anyone would graffiti the coffee shop. You reported a body? So, what? That's what yer supposed ta do. Why would anyone take that out on you, ya know?"

"You're right." I urged him with a go-on look. "Why was the coffee shop targeted?"

He smoothed back what was left of his hair and shrugged. "You have an idea?"

I took a short while to consider it. "Maybe her competitor in the contest wanted to make the coffee shop look bad?"

"Or, just kids makin' trouble," he offered.

"That sounds about right, too," I agreed. "Or the killer wants me discredited as a witness?"

"Killer? What's this?" He seemed to swell up as he stood next to my truck. "Someone hassling you?"

"No! No, no, no." I waved my hands all around. His protective self was making an appearance. "Nothing like that."

"Other than the vandalism."

"Yeah, other than that." And the article, too, which came out first. Then the graffiti happened. The words were aimed at me, not Kris, even though it was her shop that was tagged. Someone was trying to cause me trouble, but I didn't want the old man to worry about me, so I said, "Thanks for listening, Old Man. I should be going."

"You be careful," he warned me as he stepped away.

"I will."

"And don't you go worryin' about what other people think."

"I won't."

"Because you're an honest, hardworking, wonderful person, Delaney."

"You're right. I'm fantastic." I laughed.

I hoisted myself into my truck cab and shut the door. Byron waited until I fired up the engine before he returned inside the autobody shop. I blew out a breath as I exited onto Fifth and followed that to Main.

Soon the city streets were behind me and I found myself surrounded by rolling fields and trees, looking for broken-down vehicles. I relished the smell of the mountains and the fresh pine needles in the crisp air. The blue-painted sky was interrupted by snow-white peaks and a few streaks of white cloud.

Affixing my phone's earbud to my ear, I spoke into Bluetooth to call Officer Bowers. When he picked up, I said, "Zach, it's Delaney."

"I know why you're calling. Road's still closed, but the plows have started clearing the snow."

"Good. I was wondering if you were able to get more information from that webcam you told me about?" I steered around a curve and stared at the empty road.

"Yes, I did. The webcam didn't catch any vehicles going west up the pass, but there was a vehicle eastbound coming down ahead of you. He reached the bottom about four hours before you did. Nothing after you, of course, because the gate was closed by that point."

"So there was at least one other car on the pass. Other than the woman's, that is." A great leap of excitement raced around my stomach. A witness. Or killer?

Zach went on. "I caught the license plate and called the registered owner to confirm he was the one on the webcam."

"What did he say?" I slowed down and steered my truck onto the shoulder to idle.

"He didn't see any cars on the side of the road. He didn't see any other cars at all, going either east or west. I asked him if he was certain, and he explained that he was looking for unstable snowpack and keeping an eye on the weather. He came off as a snow geek. I trust his observations."

I mentally added the snow geek to my suspect list of one, counting him.

Zach added, "The guy said he went over the summit around ten. That's where you think you saw the stall, right? He didn't see it."

"Okay. So, the woman had to have reached the top of the pass after he did and before me, of course. I spotted her car there around two. So whatever happened happened in that window of time. And that would put the time of death between ten and two."

"Right now we don't have any confirmation that a woman died. Even so, someone could have dumped a dead body. We would need a coroner to estimate time of death," Zach said. I could imagine the eyeroll. "I hope you're satisfied that we've checked out this lead."

"Isn't there anything more you can investigate?"

"Like what?"

"Are there any other webcams?"

"No, there's no other webcam. No other camera to check. We've done everything we can."

Man, if this was all the cops were doing, time was

wasting away, and I might as well try to ask questions on my own. "Can I get the name of the snow geek?"

"No, Delaney. I'm not giving out anyone's name."

"Okay, okay," I said in a sing-song voice, but added, "Thanks for telling me this."

I double-tapped my earbud to end the call, an anxious feeling skirting the edge of my thoughts. I wanted the woman found. Not just for my own validation, but for her sake, and her family's sake. Someone must be worried about her.

My phone rang and I answered to a woman who needed her Tesla towed from the mall, so I pulled back onto the pavement. There were no stalls on this empty road anyway.

The shopping center parking lot was full of Fords and Chevys out the wazoo. Hers was the only Tesla and it was parked at the VIP spot near the mall entrance. Not only was her car conspicuous, her long twill jacket, stylish jeans, and suede boots caught my eye, too. She explained her car trouble and told me where she wanted the Tesla towed. Once she stood to the side, I trundled the tow dollies to the Tesla's back end and pumped them up with the foot lever to lift the rear wheels.

My customer watched with interest. "Can I video this?" She waved her cell phone in small circles.

I gnawed on my lower lip. "Why would you want to?"

"I thought tow trucks had a hook on the end, but yours doesn't. It's fascinating to see how yours works."

Her request seemed a little suspicious.

"My truck is a self-loader, not a wrecker with a hook."

"I guess I've never paid that close of attention

before. I want to show my friends. They'll want to see this." She held up her camera. "I videotape everything. Pretty please?" She must've sensed my reluctance because she added, "I'll give you a good review and recommend you to anyone looking for a tow."

A good review?

A recommendation?

I could use the promotion. "Well, all right."

I reversed my truck to the front of the Tesla and pressed the button on the remote. With the whine of hydraulics, the T-shaped bar lowered to the ground, the crossbar extended, and the claws rotated around the front tires. Another swish and hiss, and the boom raised the front of the target off the ground. The dollies lifted the back, the boom elevated the front.

My customer had a lot of questions, including how I got into the business and learned the trade. I was smiling to conceal my nervousness, but explained that hauling cars was not simple. The driver had to know if the vehicle was front or rear-wheel drive. Electric cars like the Tesla have towing limitations; they can't be flat towed due to the regenerative charging system in the wheel hub/brake system. Teslas are treated like an AWD which requires both wheel lifts and dollies. If it needs to be rolled or winched…and the Tesla is dead, the entire car is inaccessible and…just take it from me. It's complicated.

Sometimes I amaze myself that I know this.

She handed me her credit card. "Your legs are so toned. Do you work out? I hope you don't mind me mentioning it."

"Not at all." I laughed and swiped the plastic on my smart phone. I was wearing red four-inch stilettos today.

Red for power. "I don't work out, I just do a lot of squats when I release the dollies from the mounts. I'll look for your review. You'll post one, right?"

"I sure will. And I'll tell all my friends." She took my business card. Word of mouth was the best advertisement. Good reviews helped, too.

Chapter 6

Ding. Ding. Ding. My phone went off with a weather alert. Snow had started up again at the higher elevations. The roads would acquire a new coat of ice and the peaks already mantled in white would receive fresh powder. So when my phone buzzed a second time, another request for a tow, I donned my yellow work boots like the ones guys wear, only cuter, and matched the customer's location to an address.

The Nissan Juke, front-wheel drive, was stalled in the mountainside community where the celebrities lived. The woman driver sat at the curb, and I came to a stop on the other side of the street.

"Where would you like your car towed?" I asked as I alighted from the truck. The icy moisture in the air released a strong scent of wet pine needles and earth, and I wanted to believe it smelled like spring despite the snow.

"You're the high-heeled tow truck driver, but you're wearing boots."

"Bad weather, sorry. Where to?"

She told me the destination, and I motioned for her to move out of the way. I backed up to her car's front end, closing the gap, and operated the hydraulic boom.

I processed her credit card, then she buckled herself into the truck's passenger seat. With my truck's motor fired up and the heater vent blowing hot, I retraced the route back to Industrial Lane and dropped my customer and her car at the Nissan dealership.

Easy-peasy. Just like the Tesla.

Was the job getting routine and boring?

Where was the challenge?

I needed to feel the magic once again—me, the high-heeled tow truck driver with my amazing self-loader, the Xtruder. Something harder to extract would be just the ticket. Something more difficult to hook up. Some problem I hadn't encountered before...something to keep my mind off the car hidden under an avalanche, and now a fresh snowfall.

I opened the traffic application on my phone that tracked road hazards. The pass stayed closed, but a stalled car reported minutes away was worth checking out, so I performed a three-point turn around and headed for the frontage road near I-70.

When I arrived, the driver's door of the Subaru Crosstrek, all-wheel drive, was gaping open. I muscled my truck to the side of the road and killed the engine. You never know what you're going to come across when approaching a broken-down vehicle. Was this the result of a hit-and-run accident? Or a one-car accident? Was the driver inside? With horrific injuries? Had the person stumbled out of the car, or worse, been thrown out onto the side of the road somewhere? Or was it more simple? A person waiting with the door open? Waiting...for what?

I sucked in the side of my cheeks. I'd wanted some excitement. Be careful what you wished for.

I forced my steps toward the Subaru. I could do this. I would do this.

A car horn beeped. I whipped around to find an oncoming vehicle maneuvering around me before accelerating away. Jeez, people. Move over when you see a tow truck.

I edged closer to the Subaru Crosstrek until I was alongside the open door.

The car was empty. I peered in all the windows. Nothing. Nada. The only place I didn't check was the trunk.

I turned my phone over and over in my hand. There wasn't an orange tag from the city, so I had no authority to move it from the roadside. I could shut the door and leave, but walking away from this odd situation wasn't the answer either. If there was anything suspicious going on here, I'd better not touch the door or anything else.

Should I call Zach to report this? Or would he blast me for wasting his time?

I punched in his cell number.

He answered on the first ring, "What's up this time, Delaney?" After I explained what I'd found and dropped a pin to share the coordinates, he told me, "That's outside city limits. Why don't you call the county sheriff?"

I could hear his relief over the phone. "I see how you are. Way to get out of it, Zach."

He chuckled. "Can't cross over jurisdictional lines."

I left a message for Ephraim with the dispatcher, who told me he was on the way. I climbed inside my truck, feeling antsy, my mind flooded with the smells of the outdoors and the sounds of the birds. Next to the road, an icy run-off tumbled down through a rocky chasm creating a mini-waterfall. I was glad to be snug in the truck cab.

Just as I was putting the ten on the jack, an engine

rumbled in the distance and Ephraim's Clear Creek County Sheriff's truck appeared. My boots hit the ground before Ephraim was out of his vehicle.

"You said if I saw anything suspicious to contact the authorities immediately," I reminded him as he walked up to me.

"I know you called Zach first because the report came in over the radio."

"He told me this is the county's jurisdiction." I gestured toward the car. "I found it this way with the door open like that."

He strode over to inspect the vehicle. After poking his head in to look over the car's interior, he nudged the door with his foot until it clicked shut. "I'll call in the license plate and it will likely go on the tow list, but I don't think you should move it just yet."

I was right; it could be a crime scene.

"But this isn't really suspicious. There doesn't appear to be a crime, no vehicular damage, no signs of an accident, no blood. It's possible the driver left the vehicle without securing the door and it came open."

Whoops, I guess I was wrong.

I asked, "So, I shouldn't have called?"

"You can call me anytime." His gaze rested on my fingers raking through the end of my braid.

I let go of the strands and gave him an exaggerated bat of my eyelashes. "Oh, yeah?"

"Of course." He captured my face in his hands. His lips landed on mine, lingering, and a zing went to the bottom of my stomach. When we broke apart, I leaned my head against his chest and felt his heart pulsing against my forehead through his jacket. He wrapped his strong arms around me. "Call me whenever. It doesn't have to be for anything important."

"What?" I stepped back and attempted to nail him with a stern look. "Wait. Hold on."

"I meant, you can call me anytime." A few worry lines cut into his forehead.

I flung out an arm. "This car wasn't important?" Was I that bored that I was making up dangerous scenarios to keep myself entertained? Including a dead body? The body on the pass?

Gulp!

Now *I* was doing it. *I* was doubting myself. But I really did see the woman with the white face and staring eyes, honestly I did. I guess I'm not totally free of caring what people think, but I didn't need others to validate my truth. I know what I saw.

"Ephraim?" I drew out his name, a warning in my tone.

"I didn't say that. I'm glad you called. I'm glad you're being careful." He shoved his hands in his pockets.

"Is there any news about the woman I reported?"

"No. Sorry, Delaney. The plows almost made it to the top of the pass, but then it started to snow again."

My stomach muscles squeezed tight with the return of that antsy feeling. How long before the police would find her? Come on, a murderer might be on the loose and I seemed to be the only one who recognized that.

We both flinched at the sound of his mic giving out a squawk near his collar. "I have to answer this."

"Yeah, I need to go, too." I shifted my eyes back to the road.

"Want me to bring dinner over tonight before the movie?"

Friday night was our date night and we'd made plans to see a film. "Depends. What kind of dinner?" I was still acting all grumpy.

He leaned over and gently brushed his lips against mine. "It'll be a surprise."

In other words, he would decide on his way to my place. We simultaneously got in our vehicles. I pulled out first with Ephraim behind me, then I lost him at the intersection so I double-timed it back to Oberly Motors. It felt like I was done for the day, and I knew Axle was planning to cut out of work early, too.

Inside the first bay, a Range Rover, available in both front-wheel and four-wheel drive, was up on the rack and Axle's overalls were splattered with paint.

"I thought you were leaving early today?" I asked. "Don't you have to practice with the band?"

"Yeah, I'm finished here." He removed his protective eye covering. "Don't touch. It's still wet. It's amazing, huh?"

"Pretty."

"You want to catch a ride from me? I have the Altima up and running."

I laughed. "Imagine that. One for the weird files." But I'd have to leave the Fiat here where I'd parked it while I had the truck out all day. "I'll need a ride back over here in the morning."

"No prob. Go talk to Byron while I clean up." He walked over to the sink.

I went into the lobby but Byron was on the phone, so I just waved and went outside to stand next to Axle's Nissan Altima, front-wheel drive. Finally Axle loped across the pavement, wireless buds in his ears and minus his paint-splattered coveralls. I barely had time to buckle my seat belt before we sped out of the parking lot. I was just about to yell at him to slow down when he hit the brakes and I bounced against the seat belt.

"Thanks for letting me know the whole band needed to sleep in our apartment last night. What happened? Why was everyone there?" I asked.

"We practiced late and we were wiped. Don't forget we're playing at the wine tasting room tomorrow night."

"I remember."

"And guess what?"

"The music scout showed up after all?"

"No. I wish. Guess again."

"No idea, li'l cuz."

"Boss got out this afternoon. He just shot through the door. What if he runs away?"

My heart clenched as I thought about it for a second. There were all kinds of dangers in the nearby forest. Like wild animals. Like bear. Dread raced around my veins.

I frowned. "What's the matter with that dog?"

Axle, not wearing his usual beanie, ran a hand through his hair. "I came up with a fix."

"Yeah?" I made a *speed-it-up*, *get-to-the-point* gesture. "So, what is it?"

"A GPS collar for dogs."

"How does that work?"

"A chip. You just have to download the app and it intercepts the coordinates. It displays your dog's position on a map. I ordered one for Boss. If he ever gets away, we'll be able to find him."

"Whooee. Nice one, Axle."

"If I didn't know better, I'd think you were impressed."

"Good thing you know better."

He careened into the parking lot below our apartment, and we both hopped out. I said, "I'm stopping in at the coffee shop, then I'll be up." I set off at a brisk pace toward the employee entrance.

"I'll go with you." Axle hurried to keep up. "I want to see if any of the others have made it here yet."

I slipped inside Roasters on the Ridge and went straight to the office as Axle headed toward the front. I found my Murder Board (I still believed murder was a strong possibility) and held it up to the light. Someone had scribbled circles on it like they were testing ink in a pen, and coffee rings partly obscured my crude drawings. Boss's chew marks in one corner didn't help either. Axle was busy rearranging his drum set, so I toted the board through the coffee shop and carried it up the steps to my apartment.

When I came through the door, Boss tried to dart between my legs, and I waggled a finger at him. "No, you don't." He gave up and padded along behind me as I set down the Murder Board. I rifled in the junk drawer for something to write with.

Using a marker, I added the unnamed witness Zach had discovered on the webcam, plus the time of death—between ten in the morning and two in the afternoon. I didn't want to think about the possibility that the woman had been killed earlier and dumped there. How would I ever figure that out? I stepped back to train my eyes on the board in a cop-like stare. The stick figure was particularly unhelpful, and the woman's face was fading from my memory. Kelsey's face was the one that came to mind, probably because of my nightmare.

The road report on CDOT's website still showed the pass remained closed.

I jumped into the shower and dressed in jeans and a sweater. My hair hadn't even dried before the doorbell rang and Ephraim strolled in with his butt-hugging jeans and bags of food that smelled like Chinese cuisine. Don't think I didn't notice the jeans.

After scarfing down sweet and sour chicken, we fooled Boss into thinking we were going to walk down the hall, and when he trotted in that direction we slipped out the door. Once we settled in our seats at the multiplex near the mall, Ephraim seemed to enjoy the film, but I couldn't get caught up in the story. These feel-good movies were all the same. Girl gets boy, girl loses boy, girl gets boy back. Or, boy hits hurdle, boy overcomes hurdle, boy wins all. I knew the hero wasn't going to die, so I just waited for the end. Why can't girl get boy, girl loses boy, and girl decides he's not worth it, she doesn't want the drama of it, and she goes after someone else? Or, boy doesn't overcome the hurdle and decides to go in a different direction, like becoming a tow truck driver instead of the CEO of a multinational conglomeration?

When I explained this to Ephraim on the way home, he said, "People want to see how others handle adversity and they want them to succeed, otherwise it would be boring."

"Yeah, I guess so." But these rags-to-riches stories left me thinking everyone had lofty goals but me. Mom was always reminding me driving a tow truck didn't require the college education I'd worked so hard to obtain. I never thought about college anymore and my degree in social work was gathering dust. I had worked for the Department of Social Services, but I was the tender-hearted type, tearing up at every dire situation. Those five years were hard ones, and I decided social work was not for me.

What were Ephraim's goals? He was already an awesome sheriff and had purchased his own house. Did he want to get married again? Or had his divorce soured him on marriage? Didn't he want children? He loved his nieces and nephews, so I knew he liked kids.

"What is it you want, Ephraim? And what is in your way? Like in the movie."

"Good questions. I thought about moving over to the state police. They have an office in town, but their primary job is to patrol the state highways, so that's probably what's keeping me from doing it."

So, he didn't even think about marriage and family.

"What about you, Delaney?"

Never lose at free solitaire again? Own a pair of heels in every color? Boring, right?

What I told him was, "Buy another truck. Expand the operation. Hire someone to help me." Something I'd talked about, but never managed to pull off. Ephraim only nodded; he'd heard it before. I said, "Don't forget Axle's band's playing at the wine tasting room Saturday night."

"How can I forget that? You reminded me already. And the band put up a flyer at the station. There was even an announcement on public radio."

The whole town would probably turn out for Axle. Kristen was using her marketing degree. Axle was shooting for stardom. Even Guy was going to college. And me? Nothing. I told you I was boring.

Chapter 7

The next morning, Axle dropped me off at my Fiat, and, trying to drum up some entrepreneurial spirit of my own, I showed up with a caramel macchiato at Nancy Abington's car dealership when it opened.

Nancy wasn't as warm as she usually was. I wasn't sure what was going on with her, but once seated in her office, I asked once again if she had any repos for me. Recovering vehicles from customers who defaulted on their loans paid well and was challenging.

"No, we don't have any at the moment."

"Okay, I guess that's good." I laughed. Good for her business, not mine.

"Sorry, Delaney. We'll call you when we need you. Like I told you before." She closed her eyes and took a sip of her macchiato. "Mmm, this is good." When she looked up at me she gave me a long, level look. "Any more news from Rob?" There was a harsh edge to her voice.

"No, no, just the one letter."

"That's it then?"

I took a deep breath. "Nancy, would you be terribly upset if I visited Rob in prison? Maybe he'll tell me in person what he meant in his letter, and I can put this all behind me. If you don't think I should go, I won't." I had been entertaining the idea, but kept putting it off.

Visiting someone in prison wasn't something on my bucket list.

Her eyebrows drew into a fierce scowl. "I don't think you should go, Delaney. Rob's a dangerous man. Stay away from him."

"Oh." I pushed back in my seat and hung my head. "All right."

"It's for the best."

I glanced back up. "But, you see, I want to find out all I can about my dad's death." The letter I'd received from the estate attorney with the news he'd left me his tow truck was a bit of a shock. His death robbed me of the chance to know him. I had so many questions, including what caused his accident and why he had to die when I still had so much to figure out.

She picked at one of her manicured nails with downcast eyes, then let out a sigh. "Okay. What do you want to know?"

"Is there anything you can tell me? Any reason Rob would say you have information for me? I mean, what would prompt him to say that?" I hoped it wasn't just to cause trouble for his ex-wife and deflect suspicion from himself.

She rubbed a temple with one finger. "All right. This might be what he was referring to. A car was stolen from the dealership. It was found and returned with damage."

"This was around the time of my dad's death, I take it?" When she nodded, I wanted to pump my fist in the air but refrained. Maybe I shouldn't get too excited about this news yet. "So, the car was in an accident. Why didn't the police connect it to Dad's hit and run? I would've heard about it if they had."

"Well, it was found near the dealership by one of my

employees. We just repaired it without police involvement."

My heart dropped. "Why would you do that?"

"I honestly didn't think about your dad's accident. The car was found less than a mile from here, not anywhere near where your dad's car went off the road. It couldn't have been involved in the hit and run."

I came close to groaning. "But you don't know that for sure."

"I'm sorry, Delaney. Looking back, that was the wrong thing to do. That's why I didn't want to mention it."

"Can you at least tell me what kind of car? Color? Make, model, year?"

"I don't remember. And we didn't keep records once the car was sold at auction." All business now, she added, "Someone will call you as soon as we have a repo. You'll be hearing from us before long."

My stomach was as heavy as an engine full of lead, but I told her thanks before clicking down the hall and out the door in my high heels. Did I believe her? Wouldn't she keep more detailed records of cars passing through the dealership? I swallowed against a tightness in my throat as I drove back to my apartment.

Once I'd parked my car, I checked my phone. A road report had popped up on my screen. "Clarkson Pass Open. Avalanche Cleared."

I called Ephraim. "The pass is open."

"I heard."

"Any news on the body?"

"You'll be the first one I call."

"Good to know." I stabbed the phone to disconnect. I raced to pick up the truck, then sped over to I-70 and headed up the pass. I navigated the sweeping turns, where broken branches littered the side of the road and melting snow streamed down the mountain runoff. I cracked the window to let in the blowing air, and the wind caressed my face. Before I got very far into the switchbacks, an ambulance without emergency lights passed me going the other way. I hooked a U-turn at the next pull-out and followed the ambulance to the hospital.

It was hard to get too excited over someone else's misfortune, but everyone would have to believe me now.

I asked the emergency room receptionist about the patient in the ambulance. She told me, using a slow polite voice, that she could not give out that kind of information. My cell rang and I picked it up.

"Delaney, the victim was found," Ephraim said by way of greeting.

"I know."

"How'd you find out?"

"I saw the ambulance and followed it to the hospital."

"I'm at the hospital. Hold on, I see you." The phone went dead as Ephraim strode up to me. "So, you chased the ambulance?"

"I guess. Do you know who she is?"

"Registered owner of the car is McKenna King. The victim matches the picture on the driver's license in her purse, so we're pretty confident that's who she is, although she will need to be officially identified. She was only twenty-one." He shook his head sadly.

"How did she die?"

"Looks like blunt force trauma, but the coroner will make that determination."

"Trauma from a car accident? The avalanche?"

"No and no."

"Murder?"

"It's still under investigation but it's looking that way."

Even though my suspicions were confirmed, there was a hollowness in my chest. I was vindicated, but now I wished it wasn't true. McKenna was younger than me by seven years, her life was deliberately cut short, and it seemed such an appalling waste.

"You were right, Delaney, she didn't die a natural death. I should never have doubted you."

"Excuse me?" I huffed out a breath.

"I need to talk to the pathologist. I'll call you later." He walked briskly down the hallway and turned the corner. I went back to my truck and sat in the driver's seat.

Now we're getting somewhere. I couldn't help but feel outrage at the person responsible and a deep desire to know exactly how, when, and why this young woman was murdered. Maybe this was a mystery I could figure out.

Opening my phone, I found plenty of hits on the internet for McKenna King, in spite of her name being unusual. A pharmacist, a teacher, an award-winning something-or-other. One had a private social media page with a public profile picture, and I pinched my phone screen to make the photo larger.

Then I stared at it in open-mouthed astonishment.

The full-of-life face in the photo was quite different from the white wide-eyed face of the dead woman I remembered, but it was her, an animated version of her. This photo showed a living and breathing person, a stark contrast to the dead woman's dull, staring eyes and lack of expression…and it was definitely the same person. Barely recognizable, but the same. And the woman's happy smiling face in the profile picture…was familiar to me.

She looked just like Kelsey.

The singer in Axle's band.

The similarities were not apparent when I had only the lifeless face to compare to Kelsey's. But now, it was obvious; the two women had to be related. What other explanation could there be for the unlikely doppelganger?

I put the truck in gear and drove to the wine tasting room where I knew the band would be setting up for their gig tonight. The Yarborough Winery was located at the corner of Tall Chief Road and Bald Eagle Way in a building that had once housed a gas station. The garage doors were designed to be rolled up during warmer temperatures, but they were pulled all the way down today with condensation obscuring the glass.

When I walked inside, Axle sat behind his drum set, Mace and Justin slouched in chairs at the nearest table, and Barlow, the stalker-fan or STAN as Axle called him, was at the wine bar. They all displayed a dazed stupor, and Kelsey wasn't there.

I walked up to them. "Where's Kelsey?"

Barlow leaned heavily on the counter. "She got some bad news and had to leave."

"What happened?" As if I didn't have a guess.

"Her sister died. She's meeting her mom at the hospital."

I sank down at the table with Mace and Justin and faced Barlow. "Is her sister's name McKenna?"

He nodded.

I asked them all, "Did she tell you her sister's the one I saw on Clarkson Pass?"

"No." Justin pulled a hand down his face. "The dead body was for real?"

"Yes." I tried to keep the I-told-you-so tone out of my voice. Not appropriate after all, *amiright?*

"Holy crud," Axle said. "It's really true? And that sucks, her being Kels's sister." His voice was rough around the edges, as if full of emotion.

"What are you going to do about tonight? You still playing?" I wanted to know.

Justin answered, "We were just talking about that."

Axle said, "What if the talent scout shows up? What'll we do?"

Mace tossed his long hair around and said nothing, and I felt at a loss for words, as well. A dark blanket of grief seemed to weigh down their shoulders, like heavy snowfall on pine branches. Obviously they weren't just worried about the band. Everyone was grieving for their friend, and tears gathered in the back of my throat for the woman I barely knew, too.

"Hey, you know what?" Axle punctuated each word with a beat of the bass drum.

I took the bait. "What?"

"I got an idea." Axle suddenly grinned.

I conjured up a small smile. "Yes?"

"Why don't you take her place, Delaney?"

"What do you mean?"

"In the band." Swell, a comedian. When I barked out a laugh, he added, "You busy tonight?"

"You're serious?" My jaw went slack.

"I am." He raised the hand holding the drumstick as if swearing on it.

I said to Axle, "You're a total nutcase," and glanced at the other two. "He's serious?" Mace gave Axle a raised eyebrow but Justin nodded at me.

Axle said, "What's the problem?"

I poked the air. "You know I can't sing."

He waved away my argument. "But other than that?"

"Axle!"

"All you have to do is lip-synch. Justin has recordings of Kelsey's vocals. We can play those." That sounded absurd, but that was Axle—a teen with schemes.

I gave him a don't-be-stupid look. "You're just ha ha hilarious and I would look like a goob."

"That's never stopped you before. Come on, anybody could do it. Even you."

"Gee thanks, but no."

"Are you chicken? *Bawk, bawk.*" He flapped his arms. I was so flabbergasted by the whole idea I didn't have any more snide comments ready. Axle said, "Look, we're going to have to cancel. You want us to lose the gig? What about the music scout?"

"Noel will understand and the scout will come back another time," I protested. "Where is Noel, anyway?" Noel Yarborough ran the wine tasting room and wasn't at his usual spot behind the bar.

"In the back."

"Did he enter the restaurant contest? Is this place competing against Kris? I can't believe you'd help out Kris's rival."

"Noel didn't enter the contest. He said he didn't need the aggravation," Mace explained. "And the wine bar is not in the same category as the coffee shop."

"Oh, yeah." I nodded.

Justin said, "Talk about competition. Music's competitive. It's not an easy game to break into. You could really help us out, Delaney."

I stared from one pleading face to the other. Justin and Axle actually looked at me as if hopeful, but Mace just seemed sad. I glanced at Barlow, who had on a wide grin and two thumbs up.

He called over to me, "Do it." He put his palms together and elbows out, like in prayer. "For the band."

Justin said, "*Pleeease?*"

I was still resisting. "That'd be a hard no."

Axle's shoulders sagged in defeat. "I understand," he said, in a tone of voice that said he didn't. He turned to Justin and Mace, slumped back in their seats. "One of us needs to let Noel know we have to bail tonight."

Justin made a grave nod and a squaring of the shoulders. "I'll tell him." He placed his guitar in its case and started across the floor.

Compassion squeezed at my heart. Being in a band was Axle's dream. Playing in front of a live audience was his fantasy come true. And performing for a talent scout was a once-in-a-lifetime opportunity.

I shut my eyes and clutched the top of my head, and before I could talk myself out of it, I said, "All I'd have to do is lip-synch this one time? That's all?"

"Yes." Axle broke into a smile, threw his drumstick high in the air, and missed as it clattered to the floor. Justin came back, running over to lift me up in a bear hug before setting me back down. Barlow whooped and jumped around, punching the air. Their laughter was as contagious as herpes! Something I didn't ever want anything to do with! But I couldn't help it, I was starting to catch their excitement.

I said, "Explain it to me. The band would play live, but I'd be lip-synching to a recording? Only her vocals are taped? How's that possible?"

"Easy. Justin's a film major." Axle adjusted one of the cymbals half an inch.

Justin said, "I've been learning how to split audio files into multiple tracks. I've separated her vocals from the instrumentals. Part of an assignment for school."

Axle said, "You stand here." He positioned me on the stage. "If you hold the mic in front of your mouth, no one will be able to see your lips move, and it won't matter if your timing's a little off."

Justin pointed to Barlow, "Hey you, sit right in front. Pretend to be the audience." Barlow hustled over to the spot.

I looked out on Barlow and pictured the rest of the tables filled in. "Won't they know it's Kelsey's voice supposedly coming from me? What will the talent scout think?"

"I'll just put it out there that you two sound alike. It'll work." Justin pressed some keys on a sound mixer with sliding knobs and push buttons. Kelsey's vocals came out amplified over the sound system.

"People will notice me trying to lip synch. It's not like I know the songs. My mouth will move the wrong way."

Mace pointed to the microphone stand. "Kelsey uses a dynamic microphone. That kind requires you to hold it close for the best sound. And it's big. No one will even see your mouth."

Axle said, "Now just sort of dance up to the microphone and begin to lip-synch. Your mic will actually be off." He demonstrated by channeling Michael Jackson and skating across the stage with some fancy footwork.

OMG. Imagined hatchet to the head.

I ignored him and walked up to the microphone. Mace knelt in front of an amp and Justin pulled electrical cords across the floor. Axle played a soft *bitta-boom-bitta-boom* on the tom, then moved over to the snare, *ratta-tatta-tat-tat.* Mace took up the guitar and played a riff.

Justin said, "Sound check," and they all seemed to be listening hard.

"How's the FOH?" Axle called out while performing a solo on the snare.

I glanced at Barlow. "FOH? What's that?"

"Front of house. It's what the audience hears." He told Axle, "Drums are good."

We went over several numbers, and I did a few dance moves to make the guys satisfied. When we finished, it was almost time for their performance, and I rushed home to change. My closet didn't hold Kelsey's showy wardrobe, but I had faux leather pants, a sparkly top, and red stilettos. It was the best I could do.

I stopped at Kris's apartment to tell her. She blinked, then shook her head as if to clear her mind.

"No." Kristen grasped both my hands in hers. "You're not really going to do this. No *freakin'* way."

"Way." I squeezed her hands back. "I'll be fine, right?"

She was such a good friend she didn't answer that.

"Well, gotta run." I clattered down the stairs.

Second thoughts and dread filled my heart the moment I returned to the wine tasting room. The seating area was packed, but I tried not to look or count heads. Noel pointed me outside where the musicians were hanging around at the back of Mace's rusty VW van with Oliver Clang, the newspaper man who was also the contest judge. Mace smoked a cigarette with Clang, Axle tapped his sticks together with nervous energy, and Justin paced up and down. Inside the van, skis, poles, and snowshoes were pushed aside to make room for guitar cases and crates for amplifiers. My gaze skittered about until I focused on Clang's orange sneakers, and I couldn't keep my hands still.

Mace threw down his smoking butt. "It's time. Let's go," and the guys ran inside.

I hopped up and down in my red stilettos and screamed into my hand, "Take a breath. Chill out. It's all good."

Okay, now I was ready, but I still threw up a little bit in my mouth.

****

Exhausted after a long night of head-pounding playbacks of the night before, I woke up with dry eyes. I splashed water on my face and met Axle in the kitchen where we almost knocked heads staring at the coffee maker going *drip-drip-drip*. After the machine beeped signaling the brew was done, we collected our steaming cups and plopped onto the couch. Boss arranged himself on the sofa pillows.

Axle said, "It wasn't too bad of a disaster."

"It was a dumpster fire." The coffee was too hot, so I set my mug down.

He sniffed. "Oh, yeah?"

"Don't talk to me." I massaged my temples and tried to unstick my eyes.

"You have to admit it was funny when Ephraim showed up, and you tripped over the cords and fell backwards." There was a twitch of amusement around his mouth.

"That's so sweet, Axle. Thank you for bringing that up." I wanted to dump my coffee over the top of his head. It's a good thing it was cooling on the table a safe distance away.

"I think you have a new fan."

"Barlow Harmen?" I made a face. "I saw him videotaping me last night. You need to get that video from him, Axle."

A soft tapping on the door meant Kristen was on the other side. I recognized her knock.

I stood and stretched, cracking my back. Axle hiked up his jeans and followed me through the kitchen with Boss scrabbling along after him.

"Morning, Kris." I held the door open for her to enter while keeping Boss from running out.

"How you doing?" She gave me a quick side hug.

"I don't want to talk about it." I padded barefoot to reclaim my coffee cup and took a long swallow. "Don't bring it up. Move on."

"Delaney, it was funny. Didn't you hear everyone laughing?"

"That wasn't what I was going for. This is totally Axle's fault, by the way." I speared him with a glower while secretly scolding myself. Not a high point in my life. No wonder no one took me seriously, but at least the talent scout hadn't made an appearance. "You owe me big time, Ax."

He opened his mouth like he was going to protest, then stopped and said, "Sure, I'm down with that."

"So, tell me about Kelsey's sister, pour soul. What happened?" Kristen bounced glances between me and her cousin.

"Axle?" I looked to him for the answer.

"I dunno." He did a palm up gesture.

I sighed inwardly. "Kelsey's sister's the one I saw on Clarkson Pass. Her name is McKenna King. She died from blunt force trauma."

Kristen asked, "So, what's that mean? She hit her head or something or did the avalanche kill her?"

"Ephraim says it's early in the investigation but homicide is likely and she didn't die from the avalanche. She was dead before the avalanche hit, like I thought." I turned to focus on Axle. "How come Kelsey never said her sister was missing? I don't think anyone reported her disappearance."

A crease formed on his forehead. "Kels wasn't close to her sister. They hardly spoke."

"What about the rest of the family? Kelsey went to the hospital with her mom. Wouldn't her mom have reported McKenna missing?"

"You'll have to ask her. Not everyone is close to their mom like you are, Delaney."

That made me pause. Am I close to my mom? "So, you never met McKenna? You don't know anything about her?"

"No. And I didn't press for details." He rolled his eyes. "Kelsey's a private kind of chick. She didn't talk about her family much. We talked about other things."

"I didn't know Kelsey's last name is King."

"Yeah. Kelsey King. An awesome name." He had a starry look to his eyes.

Kristen said, "Murdered. That's terrible. Axle,

please tell Kelsey we're sorry about her sister and to let us know if there's anything we can do."

"Sure." He bobbed his head. "Oh, here's a thing. McKenna could also sing. Kelsey mentioned that." He fisted his hands and performed an imaginary drum solo in the air, then tapped his fingers on the table in complicated rhythms, then there was a long stretch of air-drumming.

I slapped his hand. "Stop that. What are you doing?"

"Playing the snare."

This time I caught his hand between my own. "You goofball."

"You are so *obnob*." Axle's word for obnoxious. He flung my hand away. "You made me drop my stick." His imaginary stick.

"You nutter." I smacked him in the shoulder.

Obviously tired of watching us exchange insults, Kristen said, hands on hips, "It is interesting that McKenna was a singer, too. You'd think the sisters would be close, having that in common."

"Who knows?" Axle leaned down to fondle Boss's ears while the dog wagged his whole back end. "You ready for a walk, buddy?" He snagged the leash off the hook and snapped it to Boss's collar. "Did you notice this?" He tugged on the leash, causing the collar to jingle. "I got the GPS collar in the mail."

"Oh, good." I hadn't noticed.

Kris squeezed my elbow. "I need to get downstairs. I just wanted to check on you. Cute video, by the way."

"Say what?" I clutched my hands over my heart.

"Your video. It's *sooo* cute, Delaney. I didn't know you were going to post a video." Kris held her phone toward me.

Did Barlow upload that video already? How could he! No, please. Lord, no. I mean, come on.

"Give me that." I snatched the phone but had trouble sharpening my eyes on the screen.

Axle ripped the phone from my hands. After a glance at it, he said, "You're pathetic."

"I know, I know." I groaned and slapped a hand against my forehead.

"No, I mean…because it's not Barlow's. It's some tow job." Axle handed me back the phone, Boss scampering around his feet, wondering why they hadn't left on their walk yet.

"Really?" I clicked on the play button and watched the short video. The woman with the Tesla had uploaded the film she'd taken, and I had to admit I looked fine in my red stilettos. My calves *were* toned. And I'd actually added mascara and styled my hair that day. It was almost like it was planned. I gave out a startled burst of laughter.

"When did you record this?" Kristen asked.

"Me? I didn't. This was taken by one of my customers." I handed the phone back to her. "I had no idea she was going to post it."

"She did you a favor. It's a nice promo." Kristen put her hand on the doorknob.

"Really? You think so?"

Axle said, "Almost ten thousand views already."

"*Shuddup.*" I did a brush-off flap of my hand, but it secretly gave me a little thrill.

Chapter 8

The highway took me across the Divide where I got off to turn back around and look for stalls in the direction of Spruce Ridge. After a few miles I came up to a man standing beside a Chevrolet Tahoe, rear-wheel drive, in a pull-off with the hood up. I angled my truck off the road, activated the LED bar, and climbed down from the cab.

"Need assistance?" I asked the stranded driver.

"Yes," the man said with evident relief.

"What's the problem?"

"All the dash lights started blinking, so I coasted to a stop. It's a diagnostic signal, some kind of major electrical issue."

"I guess you need a tow to the dealership?"

"I think I do." He read the address off his cellphone screen. "I'm lucky you came along. I called another company and they said they couldn't get here for an hour. I'm cancelling them right now." He hiked over to the edge of the gravel to make the call.

I operated the wireless remote to lower the truck's T-Bar to the ground. The scoops hadn't lined up with the wheels, so I raised the arm, backed the truck up another foot, and repeated the process. The claws went under and around the rear tires, and the hydraulic boom lifted the back of the Tahoe, swinging it into the air.

The customer came back and handed me his credit card. "You're the high-heeled tow truck driver who spotted that poor woman who died in the avalanche." He stared at the pointy toes of the gray high heels poking out from beneath the hem of my jeans. Gray for my gloomy outlook.

"The avalanche didn't kill her, she was dead already. How'd you hear about it, anyway?"

"Online, but they didn't say how she died. Couldn't you have helped her?"

"She was beyond help when I saw her. If you don't believe me, look it up. That should be somewhere on the internet, too." Feeling snarky, I shoved his card back in his hand. "Go ahead and get in the truck."

He climbed into the passenger side. Once I secured the Tahoe's wheels with tie-down straps, I jumped in the driver's seat, cranked the engine, and we sped off.

I deposited the man and his vehicle at the dealership, then meandered the north-south grid of streets until I got tired of that. I paused the tow truck just short of the gate to my impound lot at Oberly Motors to check my on-line reviews. There was nothing about what a bad person I was for leaving McKenna on the pass, like I feared, and nothing about my lip-synching performance, as I was half expecting. At least I had that going for me. I sat back in my seat and let out a long breath. I decided to finish a solitaire game I'd started—it was so addictive—and played a few more until a white four-door Chevy Silverado pickup with Sheriff–Clear Creek County painted black on white pulled into the lot beside me.

I felt my face break into a smile, I was so glad to see him.

"Hey there, *hermosa*." Ephraim's head jutted out the

truck window, and two dimples appeared in his cheeks. "Sing me a song?"

"Not you, too." I slammed the driver's door to meet him at the back of my truck. "I can't believe I really lip-synched with the band."

He ran his hands down my braid, causing electricity to buzz between us. "I totally believe it."

I tossed my head back and crossed my arms against my chest. "What do you mean by that?"

"You did a nice thing for Axle. You're always looking out for him."

"Oh." I let my arms fall to my sides.

He hooked an elbow around my neck, pulling me toward him, but I pushed back. "At the hospital, you said you doubted me. You didn't believe I had found a dead woman?"

"I guess it was more like I was hoping you hadn't found a dead woman." He made a small side-to-side motion with his head.

"Hey, don't go shaking your head like that. Has anything more been determined about the cause of death? How about time of death? Any persons of interest? Any evidence?"

His lips thinned and he gave me his cop face. "We're not releasing that information."

Our eyes locked, then I broke the connection and braced myself for the routine quit-investigating speech. Ephraim almost always appreciated my insight, but he also worried that I would put myself at risk by investigating on my own. I kept my head down waiting for the lecture.

"Delaney...there's no reason for you to get involved."

And there it was.

"But I was the one who found her." My voice sounded whiny to my own ears. "I was the only one who believed she was there." Other than Kristen. And Byron, too.

"Doesn't matter. We got this covered."

"Can you at least tell me what kind of car she was driving?"

His frown deepened. "Why do you need to know that?"

I gave a dejected sigh. "I just do."

"A Subaru Legacy." His mic squawked from his duty belt, a constant interruption. "I should get going." He pressed a kiss on my lips, and then he was gone.

I powered the truck through the gate, picked up my Fiat, and secured the gate behind me before leaving. A brilliant patch of blue sky shone between the pines on the drive home. After hustling up the steps to my apartment and rubbing Boss's ears for a full five minutes, I extracted my Murder Board from the back of my closet. With my marker, I added her name, McKenna King, age twenty-one, and cause of death murder by blunt force trauma. Next I added the word *singer* and crossed out the questions that were now definitely confirmed. McKenna wasn't in a car accident, her car didn't simply stall, nor did she pull to the side of the road and freeze to death. I replaced those questions with *Who had a motive* and *what was the murder weapon?*

I printed McKenna's profile picture from her social media site, erased the stick figure and the cartoon drawing of a car, and taped her picture to the board, covering the coffee stain. It looked like Kelsey's photo was pinned there instead of McKenna's. I found a stock photo of a Subaru Legacy, all-wheel drive, and taped it to the board, too, blocking the ink scribble. Nothing else occurred to me, so I stashed the board back in my closet and shut the door against Boss.

I wagged one finger at him. "No more chewing." He pawed my jeans and gave my hand a lick.

****

The next morning, I clomped down the stairs to Kristen's coffee shop and brushed past Guy at the counter.

"Hey, I'm here!" I called to Kristen as I approached her office.

"Good morning. Look at this." She swiveled away from her computer.

"What is it?" I squinted at the website on her screen.

"A quick roaster. I just ordered it. I can roast one pound at a time and sell bags of the freshest coffee possible. I know I shouldn't be spending the contest award money before I get it, but I'll be sure to win with this new equipment."

"You'll win no matter what."

She swung back to her computer. "Next day delivery."

I thumbed on my cellphone, putting the eight on the nine, the ten on the jack.

"Delaney, did you hear me?"

"Wait a sec'." I hit auto-finish and the game ended. "Sure, I heard ya. New roaster, fresh coffee." My friend didn't usually spend money she didn't have in hand, but she must know what she was doing. "Mom's meeting me here this morning, and we're going to the mall. Any chance you could come with?" Mom had called me to confirm before she'd left her house to drive up.

"No, sorry, not sorry." Kris chuckled, and I laughed with her. Mom was best in small doses.

"No one to cover for you?" I asked.

"Not that, I want to be here in case one of the judges drops in by surprise, you know?"

"Sure, sure." How well I knew, thinking of Nic Rizzo catching me here in my pjs. I said, "I heard there's a mystery judge, a fourth one."

"Yes. It's in the rules. I told you about that, but you must've not been listening. You were playing solitaire."

I held up both hands with fingers crossed. "Well, here's to a good showing." I made my way back out front and, not being able to avoid him, gave my order to Guy.

He mentioned as he warmed my cup with hot water, "The judges haven't been in yet today, but we did some extra cleaning this morning." He filled the bottom of the cup with a shot. "Axle's band has a following. We had double our usual crowd the last time the band played here."

"Both Kris and Axle are doing so well, don't you think?" I handed him some cash and stuffed a dollar in the tip jar. I assumed Kelsey would sing with the band at their next performance and hoped no harm had been done by me at their last performance.

"Yes." He handed me my change and said, "See you later," then added as if an afterthought, "Oh, um, I meant to ask, how are *you* doing?" He worked his lips into a smirk.

"Peachy." I gave him a tight smile and followed that with a swallow of the liquid energy. He didn't mention the graffiti, and I said a little prayer of thanks for that anyway. It was long gone, all scrubbed away, old news after all.

I glanced around the coffee shop to find the typical crowd, teens joking at a table, a man and woman working on laptops, a mom with toddlers in a booth, and two men wearing shell jackets and knit caps, probably going cross-country skiing or snowshoeing after picking up coffees. Near the door, the empty plaque awaited the Top Ranked Restaurant award certificate.

I'd just turned away from the plaque when Kristen's boyfriend, Zach, walked in. I said to him, "So, Officer, I was right about the woman after all." I rubbed a fist against my chest as if polishing a badge.

"I stand corrected." He bowed at the waist.

"Smart aleck."

His chin jutted out. "You know we had to verify your sighting of the body."

"I understand, Zach. I'm just trying to lighten up the bad news."

"So, now you can stand down. The sheriff's department will take over the investigation."

I didn't dare meet his eyes. "Sure. Hey Zach, can you do me a favor?"

"What?"

I caught the hesitation in his voice. "It's about my dad's hit and run."

He perked up as if interested. "What about it?"

"I was wondering if any known car thieves or teens were arrested for joyriding around that time period?"

His forehead wrinkled with a frown. "The police would have looked for reports of stolen vehicles. That's regular procedure in a hit-and-run case."

"Oh, of course."

The door banged open, and I turned toward the entryway as Mom walked in with Nancy Abington and

Oliver Clang. Nancy was a long-time friend of my mother's, but I didn't know Mom knew Clang. The three sidled up to the counter, so I joined them.

"Hello, Laney. I'll be ready to go shopping as soon as I get my coffee." Mom gave me a quick hug, then pointed in the direction of the man with a newspaper tucked under his arm and sporting his orange sneakers, which I couldn't avoid staring at. "Do you know Oliver Clang? I ran into Nancy and Oliver on the way in. Oliver runs the online newspaper in Spruce Ridge."

"Yes, we've met." I nodded a hello to Nancy, but she didn't appear to notice. Turning her back to us, Nancy stepped up to place her order with the barista.

I pulled my gaze from the back of her head to Clang. "Are you here for the contest?" Too bad the place was nearly deserted. I wished it was full of happy customers, but the early morning rush was over. At least the shop looked spic and span and held the aroma of the dark roasted coffee. The band instruments in the corner were silent.

Clang nodded. "Every time we visit one of the competing restaurants we fill out an evaluation. So every time we're here, it's always for the contest."

"Every time?" I gulped. Had Nic Rizzo reported that he found me here after hours?

Mom asked Clang, "How many times have you stopped by Roasters?"

"A couple of times." Clang's gaze ranged over the restaurant tables. "I was snowed in at my house when the contest started, but I was here the evening the band played." He appeared to have recovered from his upset stomach from that night.

"You don't live in town?" I wanted to know.

"No, I'm up the canyon." Clang gave his order, then Mom submitted hers.

I shuffled over to the pick-up counter along with them and asked, all casual-like, "Do you live near Clarkson Pass?"

The creases deepened in his forehead. "Why do you ask?"

"Uh, just making conversation. I thought you might've been affected by the avalanche."

His face relaxed. "It missed me, but we still had about a foot of snow. I have a four-wheel pickup with a blade, so I was able to get out my driveway."

Mom fingered the necklace at her throat. "Well, Kristen makes the best, the *ab-so-lute* best, coffee in town."

The barista set their drinks on the counter and everyone reached for their cups.

Mom slurped her coffee. She slowly licked her lips, her tongue traveling in a big circle, and she rubbed her tummy. "*Mmmm.* This coffee is *sooooo* good."

What the heck? I bulged my eyes and gave Mom the silent question stare.

Clang said, "I need to get back to the newspaper office," and took off with his iced coffee. Mom asked Nancy about getting together later, but Nancy said she was busy, then she left, too.

"Mom, do you know how ridiculous you sounded?"

"I was only trying to help." She looked stricken, and I needed to cut her some slack.

I gave her an awkward back pat. "I know. That was a nice thing to do." First I was caught sleeping in the coffee shop after hours, and now Mom was behaving weird. With friends like me and Mom, who needed enemies. "Shall we head out to the mall?"

"Yes, I'm ready, Laney."

We took Mom's Chevrolet Suburban, rear-wheel drive, and went straight to the discount shoe store. First we perused the sales rack, then the regular shelves. We must have tried on ten pairs apiece. I have my dad's red hair and his name, but from Mom I get my love of shopping. And my height and petite frame (and by that I mean, we're short). And my love of shoes.

I walked out with a pair of yellow gladiator sandals. Yellow for warm weather and sunshine ahead. Spring would arrive eventually.

Several hours later and many dollars lighter, I'd left Mom at the mall and was back in my tow truck looking for break-downs and monitoring the police band radio still in use in Spruce Ridge. I needed to replenish my bank account.

I followed Pine Street to Main, then guided my truck around a curve on Columbine Drive where it turned into Green Street. A vehicle appeared to be stalled at the curb, a Toyota Corolla, front-wheel drive. Ice crackled under my feet as I stepped down from the cab onto the pavement. The strong sun would soon melt the ice.

The man staring out the front windshield didn't seem to notice me until I rapped on his window. He jolted upright as if he'd been struck by a cattle prod. The car window whirred down, and the musky scent of weed streamed out to join the breeze.

"Are you all right?" I asked, but he resumed staring into the void. "Are you having car trouble?" He didn't seem capable of answering.

I inched back a few steps and called Zach. "There's a person on the side of the road who's DUI."

"How do you know?"

"Strong weed odor, dazed, stopped at the curb."

"Not on the road, you said. Parked? Is the car running?"

"Yes, parked. No, not running."

"Are the keys in ignition?"

I leaned in to look. "No."

"It sounds like hotboxing. It's not a DUI violation and it's not an emergency, either."

"Okay."

"Why are you calling? You're losing credibility here. Again."

"Thanks, Zach." I disconnected.

I guess I won't call Ephraim then, either. I threw an uncertain look at the man in the Corolla. I can't just leave him here. Remember how I "left" McKenna? I'm responsible for this guy now.

"Do you want me to take you home? I can tow your car home, too," I said through his open window, a hand over my nose, trying not to inhale.

He turned his head toward me and his glassy eyes stared somewhere over my left shoulder. "I can walk. I live there." He tossed a thumb in the direction of a short driveway leading to an old red-brick house. He popped open his door and promptly landed face first on the pavement. I helped him to his feet and watched as he zig-zagged up the sidewalk and disappeared through the door into the house.

Who knew you had to be *driving* to be *driving under the influence*?

I didn't want to give anyone cause to doubt me again. My story about the dead woman was proven true, but Zach was not taking me seriously. Ephraim was just as bad. I couldn't expect help from either of the police officers. Not anymore. I knew the door was shut to further information, even though they both were likely aware I'd go ahead and investigate McKenna's death. My curiosity, my sense of justice, my personal involvement, my empathy for the victim and family—there were so many reasons to do this. Including the frustration I felt over my dad's unsolved death.

I squared my shoulders.

It was go time.

In spite of the bite in the air hinting that more snow was on the way, I pressed the accelerator down to the floor and pointed the truck in the direction of the highway and Clarkson Pass.

Chapter 9

I caught sight of Tanner's black oversized flatbed on I-70, and he waved one arm out his window signaling me to pull in behind him at the rest stop. I swung my feet out of the cab and met Tanner at his tailgate. We leaned against the bumper, comfortable together as fellow tow-truck drivers are.

"Where you off to?" He stood so close his minty aftershave radiated across the short distance.

"County Road 350 up to Clarkson Pass."

"You sure you want to go up there?"

"I'm going to check out the crime scene."

"That figures."

"Tanner, you believed in me, didn't you?"

He leaned in toward me and the scent of Tanner flooded my senses. "Of course, Laney. And you were proven right like I knew you would be." Tanner was the only one to call me that other than my mom. "You want me to come with you?"

My hand played with my coat sleeve. "Nah. I'll be okay."

"You're sure?"

I smiled. "Sure, I'm sure."

"Call if you need anything." He stepped away and angled himself behind the wheel of this truck. He waited for me to pull out in front of him, then we went our separate ways.

I took the exit and followed the county road made up of *S* curves that increased in elevation with each mile. Tall walls of snow hemmed in both sides of my truck, as if someone had taken a knife and cut out a passageway just for me. No other vehicles were in sight. Small flakes hit the windshield, then came down faster and faster, starting to stick. I turned on the wipers and kept chugging up the hill, the passing scenery out the window not visible behind the white flurry.

Crime-scene tape fluttered in the wind at a spot just before the summit. It's a good thing the police left the yellow ribbon or I would never have identified the spot. Between the whiteout then, the snowfall now, and the avalanche in between, nothing looked familiar. At this altitude, the temperature hovered near freezing and the icy air tingled the inside of my nose, but I took a deep breath and forced myself out of the truck.

There was nothing to see, no benefit to the trip other than recording the nearby mile marker in my notes. I snapped some photos on my cell anyway, and from the cracks in the snow coating the cliffs with white meringue peaks, another avalanche looked possible. I started up my engine with a roar, and my whole body tensed, but the snowpack held.

A three-point turnaround would be difficult because the cleared part of the road was so narrow, and I was forced to make multiple attempts by going forward, backing up, then going forward again. My rear wheels hit a slick patch, the truck fishtailed and gouged into the snowbank, and everything ground to a halt.

I tried rocking the truck forward. It was a no-go.

I attempted to back up. That should work, right?

Wrong.

The falling snow had picked up its pace. No shit? I mean, really? It was the middle of April, people!

Okay. Different approach. I pushed out the door into the bracing wind. I wiped the snow from my face and lugged out a bag of sand from the storage bin under my truck cab. Cold seeped down the back of my neck as I poured sand under each tire, then I crumpled up the bag and threw it in the backseat. Rocking the truck forward and backward once more didn't help, so I got out again and tugged the floor mat out from the passenger's side. Wedging the mat under the rear tire didn't accomplish much either; the truck was lodged too deep in the drift.

I needed a tow. Could it get any more ridiculous?

Feeling the accumulated snow on my shoulders, I practically threw myself back into the truck and grabbed my cellphone. No bars appeared. There was no service up here.

Instant panic!

My heart seized up like a motor run dry of oil.

Snow began to cover the plowed surface of the road, turning it white, like fresh powder does on the first day of ski season. Snow fell thicker and thicker, and I couldn't see the truck hood. Life had dealt me another blizzard. I swear I can't catch a break.

I struck my palms on the steering wheel five or six times and tortured myself with creative cuss words. I mean, did I really put my life at risk just so I could solve McKenna's death? After all, Kristen would win the restaurant contest. Axle would be discovered by a talent scout. But what about me? Am I really so desperate for recognition that I need to solve murders?

That mean barista, Guy, would think so.

And I'm not very proud of myself right now, either.

I'd been struggling to learn the car hauling business for a while, a woman in a man's world. This was the job I wanted more than anything else, to follow in the steps of my dad. Yet here I was, strutting around in my high heels, pretending to be a vehicle recovery specialist, solving crimes I should leave to the police. And getting myself in a predicament where I needed a tow.

I just guilt-tripped myself. At least I am amazingly good at that.

I slammed down those mental thoughts. I would be found. The pass was open to traffic. Someone would come by.

But no cell service meant I couldn't even play on-line solitaire to pass the time.

If I ran the motor, would I breathe the exhaust and end up dead on the pass like McKenna King? The woman people thought I'd fabricated? I was starting to understand how Zach could doubt me. It *was* easy to imagine things with the white landscape all around. I even thought I saw a black truck approaching.

The truck pulled up alongside me and Tanner got out. *OMG!* He was real!

I hurled myself out of the cab. "Tanner?"

"I didn't see your truck get back on I-70, and I tried to call you, but the call didn't go through."

"Thanks for coming after me." I leaned into him and his arms wrapped around me. "I tried sand and a floor mat. Nothing worked. My truck's stuck."

"We'll use my winch." He rested his chin on the top of my head and we lingered for a couple of heartbeats, then both pulled away.

Tanner was quite possibly the best tow truck driver

around, and this wasn't just me being down on myself. It was the truth. He was the one who taught me how to operate my truck. I once thought we were in love—and there were times when I still felt the spark—but Tanner's work and family priorities broke us apart. I wondered whether he had some regrets about us, but since he'd been singlehandedly raising his younger siblings after his parents died, he put his brother and sister first and his business second. I came in last, which I knew was how it had to be. And I admired him for it. His strength and capability were like a solid rock, an immovable mountain.

And never had I appreciated Tanner's ability with a tow truck and a winch more than today. Within minutes, he'd attached the cable to my truck's undercarriage and engaged the motor. The rotating spool winched my truck forward out of the snowbank. Then he retrieved the hook and rewound the cable to the spool.

He motioned for me to get back in my truck. "I'll follow you down."

I cranked the steering wheel toward the road and slowly weaved my way through the canyon with Tanner in my rearview mirror. When I drove out of the falling snow, I drew a deep breath. Before long, we were back at the rest area, parked side by side in opposite directions, open windows facing each other.

"Thanks again, Tanner. I don't know what I would've done if you hadn't showed up."

"You're a tow truck driver, Delaney. You'd have figured it out." His arm hung outside his window.

From the way my ears went hot, there was no way my face wasn't as crimson as my red boots. I laughed. "Piece of cake." Which I didn't believe for a minute.

"Take care." He thumped the side of his truck before he pulled forward and left.

Prior to becoming a tow truck driver, I'd never driven a truck. I'd never changed a tire, but I had run out of gas. I was sort of a wuss. A cream puff. And I didn't want to be that girl anymore, the one who needed a man to carry the suitcases. Although, I reminded myself, everyone needs a tow once in a while. Even me, right? Come on, that's what keeps me in business, so I ought to cut myself some slack. And solving the Mystery of the Woman on the Pass wouldn't hurt either. I couldn't help it; I needed to know.

Once home, I ran up my apartment steps two at a time. After retrieving the Murder Board from the back of my closet, I burst through the door to the coffee shop and sped into the kitchen.

As I flew by, I asked Kris, standing in front of the industrial-sized sink, "Can I use your printer?"

Her hands were plunged in hot water. "Sure."

With a whirr, then a whoosh, the printer spit out the scene photos I'd taken on my phone. I taped them to my Murder Board and wrote the mile marker next to them, fitting the numbers in the space Boss hadn't chewed up.

Kris appeared at my shoulder. "I always wondered how pictures pinned to a board helped solve the crime. How does staring at the photographs make a difference?"

I sighed. "It doesn't. I don't know what helps."

"How about the coroner's report? Would that help?"

I swung my gaze to Kristen. "You have that?"

"No, but I can get it, or the information, anyway. Zach is coming over tonight. He'll tell me if I ask him."

"I need something else, too. Someone drove down the pass ahead of me by several hours, and I need to know that person's name. Zach saw the car on a recording from a weather camera."

Kris said, "I'll find out."

Her gaze returned to the pictures, and we both stared at them a few minutes longer before giving up.

She held up the board with arms outstretched. "This can stay here." She set it on the floor in her office, and we headed to the front, lured by the smell of coffee.

Most of the tables were full of caffeine fiends working on their laptops or teenagers chatting with their friends. No one was worried about the murder near our small town. It was something that happened to other people.

When Kristen tucked herself behind the counter, Guy waved her off. "I already made your drinks." He handed Kris a vanilla coconut milk latte and me an espresso. Yes, this was another one of those two-espresso days.

She said, "Thanks, Guy, you're the best," and to me, "I need to order some product. I'll see you later, Delaney. Maybe I'll have some news tonight." Our eyes met in a moment of understanding. She returned to the back room, her latte in hand.

Guy gave me a narrow-eyed look.

I offered him my fiercest glare. "What's your problem?"

"You're messing things up for Kris."

"How so?"

"The contest. Step out of the way. I need to wait on this customer." He smiled at the woman behind me and asked her, "How may I help you?"

Guy had a few issues and rough edges, and his nasty behavior may be down to that. Kris was too nice to fire him, even though I often thought he deserved it. Kristen has a strong Christian faith, lives her beliefs, and helps those in need. I worried that people would take advantage of her, but she'd told me not to mistake sympathy and patience for lack of strength.

Hopefully the mystery judge was never on the receiving end of Guy's sharp tongue. If anyone was going to mess up the contest for Kristen, it was Guy.

My eyes swept over the room as I sipped my espresso. Could the mystery judge be here now? Who could it be? The woman in a hoodie and sweatpants on her laptop? One of the teenagers acting silly at the next table over? No, none of them. It should be someone in the hospitality industry, *amiright*? Nic Rizzo was with the Colorado State Health & Safety Department, Oliver Clang ran the online newspaper for Spruce Ridge, and Nancy Abington was a successful businesswoman. Not one of them worked in food service, except for the health department guy and that was only tangentially. Noel Yarborough operated the wine tasting room and hadn't entered the contest, so maybe he was the mystery judge, although I hadn't seen him in the coffee shop. I studied the customers again.

Barlow Harmen was seated at a table, his hair as stringy as ever. He saw me looking his way, so there was no getting out of talking to him. I walked over but didn't take a seat. "Hi, Barlow, how's your car running?" Remember, I'd towed his Chrysler PT Cruiser, front-wheel drive.

"Got a new ignition switch. It's driving fine now."

"That's good. Hey, you're not going to post that video of me lip-synching with the band, are you?"

"I haven't given it much thought."

"Please don't." I inched toward the door. "Well, it was nice talking to you."

He said, "Have you heard? Kelsey's still not coming to rehearsals."

I stopped in midstride. "I guess she's pretty broken up about her sister. Did you know McKenna?"

"No, never met her. Never saw her around. The two had a falling out when McKenna won that contest."

"A contest?" I threw my arms out and the last of my espresso sloshed around inside the to-go cup. "What's up with all these contests! So, what kind of contest?"

"Some kind of singing competition."

"Really?" I briefly wondered about that, then took a final sip and tossed my cup in the trash. "Before I go, I'm curious about the mystery judge. Do you have any idea who it is? You're always around. Maybe you've spotted someone who could be him. Or her."

"Gosh, let's see." He rubbed his chin. "Sorry, I can't say. Who do you think?"

"I haven't a clue, but I'd sure like to know. Well, take care."

Back in my truck cab, I checked the internet on my phone for any kind of competition McKenna might have entered, searching her name and the words "singing award." Up popped *Rocky Mountain High Note*, a reality television show. I clicked on a video of McKenna King's performance for which she won the grand prize of a trip to Nashville to appear at the Grand Ole Opry. That was a pretty good jackpot.

Kelsey had a motive for murder. Sibling rivalry. The oldest motive there was.

I itched to write down this clue, but I couldn't write her name on my Murder Board in case Axle saw it. I feared my li'l cuz was crushing on the killer. And I was convinced Kelsey was in the running for Suspect Number One.

Since I could use a boost, I watched the Tesla video again. Several comments were posted, so I opened them. My cheeks burned when I read, "Hot chick," but my stomach twisted at the comment, "This is the crazy lady who finds dead people." Ugh.

I exited the video and punched in the number for Axle. "You done with work for the day? Want a ride home?" When he said he did, I roared my truck to life and made a beeline for Oberly Motors.

Axle waited outside while I secured my truck, then we piled into the Fiat together.

"How was your day?" I asked him.

"Fine." He turned down the music blasting through his wireless earbuds. "*Whassup?*"

"I ran into Barlow, and he said Kelsey's not back with the band yet."

His face fell a little. "Yeah. We're not sure if she's going to come through for us."

We powered past Main Street, then turned onto Pine. "You know…after I spotted McKenna on the pass, I didn't see Kelsey at Roasters playing with the band."

"She couldn't practice that night. She had something else goin' on."

No alibi?

I trod carefully, using an upbeat tone. "So, did you know McKenna won the grand prize in that TV show, *Rocky Mountain High Note?*"

His face puckered as if in thought. "I never heard of that show."

"If you win, you get a trip to Nashville to perform at

the Grand Ole Opry."

"That'd be amazing. Our band's not country western, but Nashville's the place to be. All types of performers want to play there."

I took one hand off the wheel to tag him in the shoulder. "You should try out. Or the band should, I mean."

"I wonder how Kels would feel about it." Axle's eyes rounded. "Oh no, oh no, you don't. You think Kelsey murdered her sister because of the show?" He gave me a now-you're-going-to-get-it look.

Uh-oh. Major goof.

"I never." I totally did, as you know. And since Axle was aware, I might as well add Kelsey's name to my Murder Board after all.

"No *cap*! You *do* think Kelsey did it, but there's no way. No frickin' way."

"All right, all right—"

He held up a finger like *stop talking.* "Remember, innocent until proven guilty."

"Good point," I said, giving up the argument. "What about Barlow? He seems to know a lot about the sisters. He knew about the contest. He told me he never met McKenna, but he could be lying about that."

Axle shrugged. "He's more likely a murderer than Kels."

"His motive would be...he's an obnoxious fan?"

He gave me another shrug, jerking his shoulder up and letting it fall back down.

"So, can you think of anyone else? Barlow...and?" I refrained from adding Kelsey.

"That's all you got?"

"I knew you'd be interested."

"I'm not."

"You are, too."

"Not."

I parked the Fiat in the lot below our apartment and trailed Axle up the stairs. I whispered at his back, "Are, too."

Chapter 10

In spite of Nancy's warning not to go and in spite of agreeing with her that it was a bad idea, I turned into the prison parking lot and steeled myself to go inside.

Razor wire surrounded the formidable cement-block building with armed guard towers at each corner. I'd signed up for a visit over the web and read through the instructions, so I was as prepared as possible. I had my ID but no weapons. A no-brainer, but I suppose some people had to be told.

I got in line at the visitor's entrance, waiting among other desperate-looking people, our feet stepping over tossed cigarette butts, then proceeded through security. We were all told to remain seated in a large gray room of orange plastic chairs. Unpleasant smells like boiled spaghetti, dusty metal, and lemony disinfectant scented the air. Most of the visitors were young women, but some appeared to be middle-aged, or they just looked older than their years.

My palms were slick, and my stomach did a flip when we were all instructed to rise and walk single-file into the visiting area. I shuffled along with everyone else to enter a large room of tables divided by glass partitions with phones for communication. Rob Abington waited for me at one of the tables, and I took the chair on the other side of the glass opposite him. He looked like a shell of his former self, like he'd aged twenty years. The lines on his forehead and around his eyes were deeper, his eyes sunken, and his brown hair had turned gray. Bitterness seeped from his pores.

We picked up our phones.

He asked, "Why are you here, Delaney?"

"Is our conversation being recorded?" I leaned my elbows on the hard, cold metal table. The room was chilly but held an odor of sweat.

"No, but we are being monitored by the guards." He inclined his head toward a nearby man in a uniform. Several others were stationed around the room without windows.

"Nancy told me a car at the dealership went missing. It was later found with damage. Was that the car in my dad's hit and run?"

The muscles in his jaw flinched. "I shouldn't've said anything about Nancy. She doesn't know anything."

"But you said she did."

"I was wrong."

What kind of game was he playing? I said softly into the phone, "She knew about the chop shop?"

"What chop shop?"

"Come on, Mr. Abington. She told me about the stolen car. She knew about that." When his lips remained pressed together, I guessed, "Is my dad's death connected to L&B Garage? Or the car dealership?" I'd always wondered in the back of my mind whether Dad was somehow involved in Rob's illegal activities. I didn't know Dad well enough to be sure. I told myself it wouldn't matter if he was, he'd still be my dad, but hoped he'd been an honest person.

Rob's voice dropped to a whisper. "Leave Nancy

alone, do you hear me? I still have power in that town."

I supposed I should be afraid. This place was intimidating. But the man across from me was incarcerated. What power could he actually wield from here? Spruce Ridge was a dot on the map, and the truth was, Mr. Abington was a small crook from a small town.

I asked, "Why would you write to me telling me to ask Nancy about the accident if the stolen car was not the one involved?"

His jaw stayed set in a hard line. "I said to forget it. Why I even answered your letter, I don't know." He hung up the phone and held up a finger signaling he was done. One of the guards came to collect him, so I pushed my chair back and made my way out of the room.

I'd told no one I was going to visit Rob today. Byron wouldn't have approved. Kristen might've thought it a nice thing to do, totally missing the point. Axle wouldn't've had time to come with me. Ephraim, on the other hand, probably would have accompanied me, but I felt this was something I wanted to do on my own. And of course, I hadn't told Nancy.

****

"What smells so good?" Axle had been holed up in his room, but he'd followed his nose to the kitchen.

Although the pantry was getting bare, it held the ingredients for pork green chili, so I'd defrosted a couple pork chops, cut them into bite-sized pieces, and browned them in the cast iron skillet. Next I'd dumped in black beans, chopped tomatoes, green chilis, cooked brown rice, a generous shake of cumin, and topped it all with shredded cheese. The skillet was in the oven.

I was my mother's daughter, and she was the queen of comfort food, which I needed tonight.

"Dinner will be ready in thirty minutes." I set the table while Axle practically danced around with impatience. "Go knock on Kris's door, why don't you? See if she's hungry."

Axle whisked out and back with Kristen in tow. Boss tried to race through their legs, but Axle grabbed hold of his collar. Kris had the Murder Board in her hands.

Ax said to me, "You got Kris roped in, too?"

"She sure did." Kris laughed. "I grabbed this from my office. Remember, I told you to leave it there."

"Yeah, deal with it, Axle." I propped the board on the counter and wrote the word *Suspects* with both Kelsey's and Barlow's names underneath. Why not? I didn't have a whole lot of names to consider.

"The killer's not Kelsey, Delaney," Axle said.

"I just need to eliminate her then. I wonder where I can get a picture of Barlow?"

"I have one." Axle thumbed his phone and brought up a picture of the band with a clear Barlow photobomb. "Sent to the printer." A clackety-clack, then a whoosh could be heard from Axle's room. He ran for the photo to pin it to the board where he wrote, *Stalker? Not a good motive.*

The oven dinged and the three of us grabbed plates.

After a few bites, I asked, "What about Justin or Mace? Were you with them all that day?" I pointed to where the possible time of death was written next to the coffee stain—between ten in the morning and two in the afternoon.

"No, we all met at Roasters at four."

"Maybe the killer avoided the webcam somehow." I explained the weather camera recorded only two vehicles coming down the pass during the pertinent window of time, mine and one other. "Did you find out about that driver?" I asked Kris.

"Not yet." She glanced at her watch. "Zach's not off for another hour."

I scraped a generous helping of green chili onto an extra plate and covered it with foil. "Take this with you. He'll be hungry."

Kris left, and Axle and I stared at each other. He asked, "Why would Justin or Mace kill Kelsey's sister? None of us knew her sister. Even Barlow's a stretch."

"I don't know. But I'm going to include them anyway. You can help me eliminate them as suspects." I walked over to the board to write their names with question marks for motives. Mace's and Justin's faces were alongside Barlow's in the photo of the band.

"I'll ask them about it." He rubbed the beanie that covered his head.

"Aw, Axle...you *are* going to help me." I gave him a smile.

"Yeah, you might need some help."

There was no *might* about it. I totally needed help. "I'll leave the Murder Board here. Feel free to write on it if you can find room." Between my scribblings and the ink circles where someone had tested a pen and the dog-chewed corner, there wasn't much space left.

"So, Kris is going to ply Zach for clues?" Axle popped his earbuds out of their case and screwed them into his ears.

"He likes to talk about work."

"I'm sure that's not all he likes. Should we go over and pound on the door?" He laughed.

I put my hands over my ears. "I can't hear you."

"Maybe send her a text your mom's on her way up the stairs and wants to talk to her. We should totally do that." Axle threw back his head and laughed even harder, apparently lacking good judgment.

"What's wrong with you?" I shook my fist. "You twerp."

"Fine," he smirked. "I see how you are, no fun."

"You know what would be fun? How about you ride along with me on my next tow? You haven't done that in forever."

"I've been busy with the band."

I struggled against disappointment. Just then, as if thinking about work conjured up a customer, my phone rang. A Hyundai Genesis, all-wheel drive, stranded. Axle went to his room while I gathered my boots and coat.

When I got back from taking care of that job, Axle was gone—practicing with the band somewhere—but there was a note under the door that I brought inside with me.

Written in Kristen's handwriting was: *The avalanche didn't disturb the evidence, her car was intact, the frame not compromised. She wasn't crushed. But the cause of death was a blow to the head sometime prior to the avalanche. Her fingerprints on the steering wheel showed she drove there, and blood spatter indicated she was in the driver's seat when attacked, so not killed elsewhere.*

So my estimated time of death was correct, between ten and two. It had to be if she'd driven herself to the summit. The question of whether she'd been killed earlier and dumped there was answered. She hadn't been. She drove herself. But why did she stop at the summit?

What happened to the killer? How did he or she get away?

At the bottom of the note were the words, *Kabir Bhatt*. When I searched the internet, I figured out that was a name, and since it was an unusual name, I also located an address.

****

Tuesday morning found me zooming my Fiat down I-70, past Morrison with the hogbacks, past Red Rocks Amphitheater into Golden, along Highway 93 toward Boulder, then past the former site of a nuclear power plant, now long gone. The brown prairie undulated to the foot of the mountains, crisscrossed by recently built neighborhoods with green grass and trees.

Kabir Bhatt lived in an upscale home between Superior and Boulder. His wife answered the door and told me he was at work, but gave me his cell number when I explained why I wanted to talk to him. He agreed to meet me at a coffee shop, and I mentioned my red hair and pink stilettos. Can't miss me. And a coffee shop would be a safe public place.

When I walked inside, the comforting aroma of coffee reminded me of Kristen's café. A suited man at the table with a coffee mug in front of him waved, and I stepped over to him. "I'm Delaney Morran, Mr. Bhatt."

He politely stood up, held out a warm hand for me to shake, then when I sat, he sat, too. "Call me Kabir. The police already talked to me about the day I drove over Clarkson Pass."

"I know, and thanks for meeting with me. I'm sure the police also told you about the woman who died."

"They said there was a report of a body." He nodded. "And I saw on the news that the body was later found."

"Exactly. I'm looking for a few more details. What time you were near mile marker—" I looked at the note on my phone. "—140? It's close to the top."

"Let me see." He opened the camera app on his phone and flipped through pictures, then swiveled his screen in my direction.

After viewing a few photos, I recognized the spot from my recent visit to the crime scene. "Oh, wow. You must've stopped right at the place where the woman's car was parked. This picture was taken before she got there."

He pinched the photo to enlarge the image as we studied it together, along with the ones taken just before and after. No Subaru Legacy on the shoulder, but the snowpack was cracked, a warning sign for an avalanche. He said, "It shows I took that picture at 11:36."

I made a note. "Did you see any cars on the road?"

"I didn't."

"No Subaru Legacy?"

"No. No vehicles. Sorry."

"Why did you stop at that particular point?" I toyed with my pen.

"The snowpack was showing vulnerability at that location."

"You're interested in the weather?" A weather geek was what Zach called him.

"I work for NOAA, so it's more than an interest."

"Oh, I see." I absently touched my thick braid. "Can you tell me about the webcam at the bottom of the pass? It's a NOAA cam?"

He explained that the camcorder was pointed at the atmosphere, and the road could only be seen in one corner of the frame. "The images are amazingly clear, but if precipitation gets on the lens, it could obscure the image for a minute or two. Plus, the webcam can have glitches. It's not meant for surveillance."

"Okay."

"Is there anything else I can do for you?"

"Can you send me the pictures you took at that mile marker?" I gave him my cell number. He poked his phone screen and my phone dinged with a text received.

Now I had more photos for my Murder Board. But what did that get me? More images to stare at. At least I'd learned the woman was killed after 11:36. She was there, dead, when I drove past around two.

I'd narrowed the window for the time of death a little bit more. I was whittling it down.

And the webcam wasn't foolproof.

Even though Zach seemed to believe no one else was on the road, someone could've slipped past the camera when the lens was wet or during a recording glitch.

I thanked Kabir before leaving. He'd been so helpful, it was unlikely he was the killer. Plus his photos proved the Subaru was not there when he was.

On the way back up Floyd Hill, with the mountain tops hidden behind a haze, I received a call from Ephraim. "Hi, *bella dama*," he said when I answered on Bluetooth. "You have time to meet for lunch?"

"*Ohhhh,* yeah. Where?"

"You pick. I just need a quick bite. Somewhere close to work?"

"Bagel sandwiches at the coffee and bagel place across from the sheriff's station?"

"Perfect."

Zach was certain to have provided the webcam footage to the county sheriffs—Ephraim and his investigative team. Was Ephraim looking for other drivers? If not, where else was he looking? Who was he talking to? Maybe I'd get the chance at lunch to ask Ephraim for information. There might be an opening, and I'd be ready to take it.

I arrived first and snagged a booth. The deli counter displayed specialty cream cheese spreads, other sandwich fillings, and a variety of bagels. The waitstaff brought me two menus and waters, and I played some solitaire on my phone, nine on ten, eight on nine, move the king over, and the queen on the king.

When the door opened, I peeled my eyes from the game. The three restaurant judges, Nancy Abington, Nic Rizzo, and Oliver Clang, took a booth across the room. I hid behind one of the menus and stared at them. They were certain to be here in connection with the contest, and this restaurant must have entered in the coffee shop category. One waiter hustled over with coffees and another took their order, all while the judges smiled and seemed to be enjoying themselves.

I took a sip of my water and managed to choke in mid-swallow. My throat prickled, my eyes watered, and I coughed, gasping for air. "*Hack-hack-hack!*"

The waiter ran over. "Can you breathe?"

I nodded and gave another ugly gasp. "I'm fine." My voice came out raspy. I fanned my face to dry my eyes and prevent my mascara from running. The three judges stared at me, aiming looks of alarm in my direction.

"Delaney, are you all right?" Ephraim towered over me. This was so embarrassing, I blushed, and the tip of my nose turned red, yet I managed to stifle my gag reflex and said with a hoarse voice, "I'm great." Both Ephraim and the waiter eyed me with disbelief, but the waiter took our orders and went away.

I extracted a mirror from my purse. My makeup was still intact. I dabbed the paper napkin under my eyes and added lip gloss.

Ephraim said, "You look gorgeous today."

"Thanks." I flushed with pleasure, pressing myself harder into the back of the chair.

He angled his body toward me. "So...anything new?"

Our waiter set two coffees on the table. I shook my head as I raised my cup.

"Nothing new at all?"

I took a sip of coffee and swallowed carefully. "No. How about with you? Anything new with you?"

His eyes narrowed to a straight line. "I knew it. You want to know what's new with the investigation. You're investigating."

"I am not." My face scorched hot at the denial Ephraim was sure to know was a lie. The photos I'd received from the NOAA guy sat heavily on my mind. How could I tell Ephraim about that witness now? How could I ask Ephraim for clues now? That ship had sailed.

The waiter dropped off two baskets containing our bagel sandwiches. Ephraim pushed mine toward me and handed me a paper napkin. He said, "Your video has some comments about the killer. You look real cute, by the way."

"What? What comments?" I opened the video clip of me towing the Tesla. Up to twenty-nine thousand views. In reply to the comment, *This is the crazy lady who finds dead people*, was a new post, *Maybe she's the one who murdered that poor woman. You know what they say about the one who finds the body.*

Ouch, huh?

"This is absurd." I stuffed my phone in my purse and ripped off a bite of bagel, chomping down hard. The post was anonymous. Was it posted by the killer himself?

"You can understand why I might suspect you of investigating. That, and your history..." A crease appeared between his brows.

Like, duh. How could I argue with that? I felt compelled to solve murders. Maybe if I found my dad's killer, I wouldn't be so obsessed with other victims.

Why did I give the woman with the Tesla permission to take the video? I never should have. All of a sudden my eyes pricked with stinging needles, and I blinked away the unwanted emotions.

I said, "The publicity is nice, but those comments suck."

Ephraim said, "I'm sorry about the post."

I waded up my napkin and threw it into my basket. "You need to solve this case, Sheriff, and clear my reputation."

His hand clamped down on mine. "I will. The coroner definitely ruled it a homicide. There aren't a lot of suspects, though. We've questioned the boyfriend, and he has an alibi. No one knows what the victim was doing on the pass."

I sat a little taller in my seat, reenergized like I'd just been given a fresh shot of espresso. The ship is back in the harbor. "She had a boyfriend?"

He slid his hand off mine to rub the back of his neck. "Yes, but he was a dead end."

"Who's the boyfriend?"

"He doesn't live around here. And I can't say any more about it, Delaney."

"You might as well tell me." I jabbed a finger in his direction. "What's his name? Where does he live? You're really not going to say?"

The judges' laughter reached my ears, so I stopped to watch them lingering over their coffees. Ephraim finished his last mouthful and crumpled his napkin onto his basket. I swiped the crumbs off my blouse, then we stood and went to the checkout counter where Ephraim paid the bill.

Once outside, I noticed a rusted Chrysler PT Cruiser, front-wheel drive, parked across the lot. Barlow Harmen got out and went inside the bagel shop.

I hopped into the passenger side of Ephraim's truck cab to talk a few minutes more. From the driver's seat, Ephraim leaned over to kiss me in that slow deep way that made me forget my questions. When he finally released me, I labored to breathe.

He said, "I've got to get back to work." Not the next words I was hoping for.

"Way to get out of telling me about the boyfriend." I feigned indignation.

He smiled, his teeth dazzling white in his tanned face, and turned the key to start the engine. I slid down from the cab, and he waited until I got into my Fiat before pulling out of the lot.

My sandwich had been tasty, even if I could barely eat, the restaurant clean, and the staff attentive.

They were probably in the number one spot for Top Ranked Restaurant in the coffee shop category.

I just hoped Roasters wasn't in the number *last* spot.

****

At five o'clock, I tucked my self-loader behind one of the Main Street dumpsters. While I staked out the towaway zone, I played solitaire. Time passed slowly measured by the clock on the dashboard, giving me a chance to think about everything that went wrong since I reported the body. The news article shaming me, the graffiti shaming me, the lip-synch performance, and me shaming myself. The Tesla video with the negative comments didn't help. That I need a tow—me, the high-heeled tow truck driver—when my truck got lodged in the snow on the pass didn't help. All this added up to a pretty pitiful picture. Even for me.

I shifted the truck into gear and bumped through the potholes over to the next block. A Ford Explorer, rear-wheel drive, blocked the loading zone, nose-in. *Aha, caughtcha.* I scooted my truck up to the back end and pressed the button on the remote. With the whine of hydraulics, the T-shaped bar lowered to the ground, the crossbar extended, and the claws rotated around the Explorer's rear tires. Another swish, and the boom raised the target vehicle off the ground. All this without me getting out of the cab.

I traversed the alley and turned onto Main Street. With no warning, the car alarm of all car alarms erupted—*BWEEE-BWEEE-BWEEE*—busting my ear drums. I looked in my rearview mirror while hitting the brakes. The alarm was not supposed to go off from simple contact with tires. If so, the tires would set off the alarm every time they met the road.

A huge brown blob bounced around in the front seat, jerking the Explorer up and down on the truck's boom. The blob vaulted into the backseat and pressed against the rear window. A gigantic jaw opened and ferocious teeth appeared. A loud roar, *GRRRR-GRRR-GRROOOOUUUUL* joined the car alarm in the deafening cacophony.

What the heck!

I think my eyeballs actually bulged out of my head. My heart lurched and blood whooshed in my ears.

A brown bear was in the backseat of the Ford Explorer.

What to do? What to do?

The bear scampered into the front seat and pieces of upholstery started flying. Ragged shreds of dashboard went airborne. Then the animal thrashed against the passenger window until the glass burst outward. Frankly, I was so mesmerized by the scene in my rearview mirror I just kept rolling down Main Street. The bear poked his head and shoulders completely through the window and stuck tight there, like a bear in a honey pot, and the door burst open, jutting out into traffic with the bear on board. Then the door slammed shut and popped open again, the bear sailing out and back in, seeming to enjoy the ride. A vehicle coming the other direction swerved. The driver's jaw dropped, his eyebrows shot skyward, and he accelerated off like a champion race car driver.

When the door spun open one more time, the bear launched right out through the window, went airborne, rocketing over a Ford Fiesta, front-wheel drive, and face-planted on the pavement. Caught off guard, the driver careened left and right. The bear climbed to its feet, shook its big furry head, and ambled down Main Street while gawkers took videos on their cellphones.

The car alarm continued to shriek—*bweee-bweee-bweee*—as I made a left on Fifth and the door banged shut.

Often in the spring when bears emerged from hibernation, they came into town foraging for food. The animals have been known to break into houses and vehicles. But on Main Street? Of course, the dumpsters in the alley attracted scavengers, and the bear could have gone from the trash can to the Explorer.

Once at Oberly Motors, I lowered the boom, and the Explorer's tires dropped to the ground. I jumped out of the truck and dashed toward the first open auto bay. "Axle! Axle!" I shouted over the sound of the car alarm still singing its siren tune.

He ran out with a look that said, *Say no more,* and sprang forward, diving under the front of the Explorer with only his feet sticking out.

I yelled, "Be careful."

Byron stood in the doorway, covering his ears with his hands. None too soon, the *bweee-bweee* made a final *bweee* and shut off. Blessed silence reigned, and Axle reappeared out from under the hood.

"So, what's going on?" he asked me.

"Here's the thing…" I gave him and Byron the quick version.

Axle's mouth hung open by the time I'd finished my story. "Are you *fricking* kidding me?"

"I wish."

"That is some spooky shit," Axle said, voicing my exact opinion.

I patted my chest. "I think my heart rate is finally returning to normal."

"Only you, Delaney, only you." Axle threw his hands into the air. I looked to Byron for some support, but he *tsked* and shook his head.

I raised a hand. "I'm okay. Thanks for asking."

My li'l cuz burst into laughter, tipping his head back. Then a laugh welled up inside me, too. It felt good to let it all out. The old man joined in, the sound of his laughter deep and strong in a pleasant way.

I was a little wired here, waiting for the hilarity to end. When their laughter finally wound down, and it took a while, I said, "I guess I should get back to the towaway zones. What are you two doing here so late?"

Byron answered, "A rush job. Customer needs his car back tomorrow. But we're 'bout done here, Axle, if ya want to go with Delaney."

"Actually, I decided to go home. I'm done for the night, and I'd like your company, Ax," I said in a slightly pleading tone.

He gave me an awkward back pat. "Let me get my stuff."

I operated the remote to release the Explorer from the claws and fold the T-bar onto the back of the truck. Now that the car was safely behind the security fence, I took a photo of the VIN for my records. After I parked my truck, I locked the gate behind me.

Axle walked up with a backpack hitched over one shoulder, halting his steps to pause and give me an eyeroll, then climbed into the passenger side.

"Go ahead, lay it on me. What else do you have to say?" I turned the key to crank the Fiat's engine.

"That by now everyone in town knows you towed a bear in a car down Main Street?"

"Tell me about it." I gave a tired little sigh, but he laughed so hard he needed to hang onto the door handle. "Axle, I need to talk to Kelsey. I'm thinking tomorrow."

Axle squinted one eye at me. "If you're going to do that, I'm coming, too."

I grinned back at him. "Well, that would be helpful since you probably know where she lives."

He appeared to be squashing a groan.

Chapter 11

At first I thought I'd dreamt the whole thing, but then I woke up to the headline, *High-heeled tow truck driver drags wild bear though downtown Spruce Ridge.*

The online news story included links to cellphone videos taken from different angles. Even though my pink stilettos weren't caught on film, there was a whole paragraph about my high heels.

Hey, don't disrespect a woman's shoes.

And you would think I did it on purpose.

Jeez.

The clip of the bear hitting the pavement was cringy and seared into my brain forever. The news writer opined that secret plans between property developers and social justice warriors were affecting bear activity. Whatever that meant. I was left seriously worried that bear advocates would register a complaint against me even though the bear had shaken himself off and walked away. I wanted to post the disclaimer, *No animals were harmed in the making of this film*, but farther down the page was the news that Colorado Parks and Wildlife officials had captured the bear for relocation and that the animal did not show signs of injuries. *Whew!*

I was glad for that, and at least the videos would prove to the owner how his Explorer was damaged.

I knocked on Axle's door. "Be ready in five

minutes."

It took Axle longer than five to eat his cereal and check his texts, but we finally descended the stairs. On the way to my car, we stopped in our tracks.

My Fiat had been vandalized in the night.

Axle said, "Wow. Just wow."

The words, *Stiletto zero, Bear won*, covered the windows and windshield. I scraped my fingernail across the writing on the glass and soap curled away. Since cigarette butts dotted the pavement under my car, this looked more like the work of teenage smokers who couldn't spell than a serious threat.

Axle went back inside for window cleaner and paper towels, and together we had the graffiti cleaned away in no time.

Once on the road, Axle told me, "Shake it off, Delaney."

"Okay." I gave him a sideways glance.

"Hey, I called Kelsey. I told her we wanted to stop by on the way into work." Axle had on a self-satisfied smirk. He'd warned her about our visit when I'd hoped to catch her by surprise. He said, getting out his phone, "And I gotta let Byron know I'm going to be late today." He got busy texting.

"Well, thanks for coming with me, Axle." At least I wasn't doing this on my own.

The wind was chilly with the lingering undertone of rain as we motored over to her house, a small ranch near the historical district. Waves of aftershave preceded Axle up the sidewalk, and Kelsey twitched back the curtain when we knocked on the door.

"Hi, Ax, Delaney." She ushered us into the living room. "You want something to drink?"

"Yeah. I could sink a beer." Axle plopped onto the couch, not meeting my gaze. He was underage and it was nine in the morning, but I wasn't about to squelch my li'l cuz.

I said, "Nothing for me. Thanks."

When Kelsey left for the kitchen, I mouthed, "Beer, Ax? Really?" He shrugged.

I moved around the room with antique-looking furniture and dusty paintings of mountain scenes in heavy frames. There were no family pictures or anything else of interest, so I slid open a drawer to the sofa table and peeked inside.

"What are you doing?" Axle jumped up and gave my arm a sharp pinch.

I rubbed the spot. "Keep up, here. I'm looking for clues." I went to the bookcase and pulled out a book to rifle through the pages. Nothing hidden there.

"Be devious. You're good at that," Axle said over my shoulder, practically stepping on my heels.

Not finding anything, I whispered, "After you drink your beer, ask to go the bathroom and check her medicine cabinet." Detectives on TV always checked there for drugs.

"Pass on that," he said in a loud voice.

I gave him the shush sign, "*Shhhh*," and searched in the television cabinet, picking through the remote controls. We both froze when we heard Kelsey approaching. When she entered the room with two opened longneck beers, Axle was sprawled back on the couch and I was relaxed in a wingback chair, all nonchalant-like.

She handed Axle a beer and took a seat on the sofa next to him.

I said, "I'm sorry for your loss, Kelsey. I should've mentioned that first thing."

"Thanks." She glanced at the floor with a frown. "Axle probably told you I wasn't that close to Kenna."

I nodded. "Have the police told you anything?"

She snapped her eyes back up to me. "No, not really." Her eyes weren't red. No sign of tears.

I took a steely breath. "I heard McKenna's boyfriend's been cleared. He has an alibi."

Her head dipped in a nod, but her face clouded over.

I asked, "Do you know whether the police have any suspects?" Kelsey shook her head. "Did she have any enemies?" Her head shook again. "Did you ever sing together? Were you in a band together?"

"Not really." A small, mischievous smile crossed her face. "I heard you lip-synched to my songs."

I felt heated to the roots of my hair and gave out a nervous chuckle. "And it was a disaster." I glared at Axle. "I can't believe you talked me into it."

"No one can take your place, Kels," he told her.

"What was the name of McKenna's boyfriend?" I had to ask.

"Why do you want to know? I read that article about you and the bear. What was up with that?" Her lips twitched, and I realized she was laughing at me.

Axle said, "We have a gig tonight, I hope you can make it, Kelsey. And Delaney, you and Ephraim should come."

I sent him a mental thank you for changing the subject. "Sure, sure. We'll be there. But no lip-synching for me." I was trying to be funny, but neither was listening. Axle was turned toward the woman sitting next to him, and her mind seemed to be somewhere else. Her phone emitted a vibrating sound and she drew it out of her pocket to check messages.

Axle bumped Kelsey's shoulder. "The band's looking forward to having you back. Can you make it tonight?"

"Well..." Her voice dropped abruptly. "About that..."

He tugged a strand of her hair. "What's the matter? Won't it be nice to be back?"

She gulped a breath, then said in a hurry, "I'm quitting the band. Sorry, Axle, but I need to move on."

Surprise registered on his face and he stopped in the act of lifting his beer to his mouth. He jerked his head and gaped at me.

"Is that really a good idea, Kelsey? Don't you want to surround yourself with your friends at a time like this?" I had my sympathy face plastered on, hoping to conceal my suspicion.

"I really think this is best," she said.

Silence spread through the room.

Axle had on a black look. "I need to hit the head."

Kelsey set her phone on the table. "Sure, I'll show you where it is."

When she and Axle started down the hall, I leapt up and snatched her phone. The text she'd just received was from someone I didn't know, but I spotted McKenna's name on another text, so I tapped on that. Kelsey's footsteps approached, so I quickly snapped a shot of the screen and set the phone back down.

Kelsey had only just taken her seat for a few moments before Axle returned.

I said, "Should we be going, Axle?"

He stood there like a rock, not moving. His

oversized sneakers were rooted to the spot. He was that upset.

"Here's my business card." I pulled one from the outside pocket of my purse and thrust it into Kelsey's hand. "Call me if you need anything. Please, I really mean it." I pushed Axle toward the door. "Now go on." I put an arm around my li'l cuz's shoulder and hustled him out to the Fiat. "You okay?" I asked once he'd clicked on the seatbelt and I'd pulled onto the street.

"I can't believe Kelsey quit the band." He let his head loll back on the seat and covered his eyes with his arm.

"I know."

"Why would she do that?"

"She needs a change, to move on like she said."

He dropped his arm and pointed his chin toward the passenger window. Misery poured out of him like a mountain stream overflowing its banks.

"What'd you find in her bathroom? Anything?" I was dying to know.

His shoulders slumped. "Girl stuff and a man's shaving kit."

Ahhh. Axle had had more than one letdown today. "Did you know Kelsey had a boyfriend?"

"No."

"Did she lead you on?" I stared out the windshield. I was a patient and reasonable person, but I didn't like anyone screwing around with my li'l cuz. I could see his shrug from the corner of my eye. "Did you break up with Shannon?" I asked. His girlfriend was away at college. I thought absence made the heart grow fonder, but a teenage boy might feel differently.

He countered with, "You and Ephraim ever DTR?"

My eyebrows practically launched off my head. "Ew, ew, ew!"

"You're whacko. That means 'define the relationship.' " He made little quote signs in the air with his fingers.

I said, "*Ooooh-kay*. Nice try, but I asked you first."

"We're still going out, but we're not exclusive. It's not fair to either of us." His voice was flat and expressionless.

I actually got a bit choked up, my throat tightening. Honestly, Axle never told me anything personal. Never-ever! *Nada*. Especially about his love life. This was the ultimate in drama for Axle. My heart seemed to expand and I blinked rapidly.

"That's very adult, Ax. Shows maturity."

Yeah, I can't explain that either.

He swatted the air. "Don't pile on."

"Got it. 'Nuff said. Do you want me to drop you off at work?" I asked in my best attempt to be cheerful.

"No. Just take me home. I already told Byron I'd be in later." He brought out his phone. "I need to let the band know our gig is off."

I turned such a hard left Axle's head banged into the passenger window. "Oops, sorry."

He took an instant to right himself, then started texting. When he put his phone down, he asked, "You sure you don't wanna lip—"

"No!" I shouted before he could get the words out.

"Okay, okay, don't go nuclear on me. Just thought I'd ask."

I screeched to a stop in the parking lot below our apartment and Axle shouldered open his car door. I stopped him with a hand to his arm. "That was never meant to be a permanent solution. Can't any of the guys sing the lead?"

"We'll have to practice, maybe with different arrangements. None of us have Kelsey's vocal range."

I tapped the steering wheel. "I have to run a quick errand, then I'll be right back if you need a ride to work."

"Okay." He slammed the door shut and trudged up the stairway.

I put the Fiat in gear and turned out of the lot.

The newspaper office was in a strip mall next to a tattoo parlor. Inside the tiny space, Oliver Clang sat at a metal desk. The walls held numerous framed articles and a few caught my eye. One announced, *Princess Diana's death was no accident*, and another read, *Alien crash in Area 51 uncovered*. His laptop teetered on a pile of books and, despite the newspaper being paperless, stacks of newsprint and overstuffed files littered the space. There wasn't much room to turn around.

"Can I help you?" He covered the page he was reading with a file folder.

"Hello, Mr. Clang." My eyes went to his orange sneakers poking out from under the desk.

"What are you staring at?" He pulled his feet back and sat up straight.

"Nothing. Do you have a minute to talk?"

"Only a minute. I'm very busy."

Since there wasn't a spot for a chair, I had to stand. "Your news article about me was misleading."

His face took on a wary look, as if he wasn't sure what to do with a pissed-off redhead, and he rubbed his forehead where a bead of sweat appeared. "Feel free to write a letter to the editor."

"And that would be…you, right?"

"Yes." He hardened his jaw.

"Well, I'm telling you now. This could damage my livelihood. This is very unfair and defamatory. And, you know, bear sightings are not that unusual."

"You towed a car with a bear in it." His upper lip curled in a sneer. "That's unusual."

"Well, yeah, that part."

"Again, send a letter. I'm very busy as you know. I not only run this office—" He waved his hand around as if taking in a vast empire. "—but I'm spending a lot of time judging the Top Ranked Restaurant Contest."

"What kind of a newspaper is this? You believe in aliens?" My gaze circled around the articles on the walls.

"Doesn't everyone? You need to study the facts." He stood, crowding the space and causing me to back up to the open door.

I stumbled outside, and he slammed the door in my face. I heard a lock turn.

I was kicked out of this crazy man's lair. *Sheesh.*

This was super-awk.

My phone rang just as I settled into the driver's seat of my Fiat. "Hello, Delaney? This is Nancy."

"Yes?" I clutched the phone to my ear. Was Nancy calling to give me a repo assignment? I hadn't had one lately and could use the money.

"Rob called me."

I sucked in a breath. "I didn't know inmates could make calls."

"Of course they can." Her voice sounded shrill. She was mad. "He told me you visited him. He scared me, Delaney." Now her voice quivered. "What were you thinking?"

"Sorry, Nancy, but I had to find out the truth."

"And what did you find out?"

"Nothing. He said you didn't know anything. He was sorry he sent the letter. It was a waste of my time. How did he scare you? Did he threaten you?"

"Not in so many words. I mean, the calls are monitored. Just the fact that he called was frightening. He's never called before."

"There's nothing to be afraid of. If my dad's death had nothing to do with you…" I trailed off, closing my eyes, listening hard.

"Look, mistakes were made. I need to put this behind me and you do, too."

I jumped on that. "What mistakes?"

"I don't know who took the car from the dealership that night. I should've followed up, called the police."

"Rob knows who, I'll bet." I nodded my head. "I bet Rob even gave the person the keys. That is if Rob himself wasn't the driver." I was more than willing to believe it was him, that Rob was responsible for my dad's death. He'd been implicated in a previous murder, but not convicted.

"I don't know. Maybe. But you'd need to prove it."

I had no proof. And no help from Nancy on that count. I scrunched my nose and mouthed, "Dang it," to myself. "Maybe he got someone else to do his dirty work?" He had done that before, too.

"Drop it. Please. Goodbye, Delaney." She hung up.

My car practically drove itself back to Roasters, and rolling into the coffee shop was like coming home. Nothing was going to get in the way of me and a cup of coffee. Not that mean barista, Guy. Not that stupid newspaper editor, Oliver Clang. Not that frustrating woman, Nancy Abington. And especially not that bear, a current sensation on social media. It was already coming up to eleven o'clock and I needed a cup of joe.

Guy made my espresso without comment for once, and I unpacked my laptop next to my steaming mug on the table near the window. I knew I'd made the right decision when after one breath of the aroma, already I felt calmer. A drizzle of rain had started up and lashed against the glass. First up, Oliver Clang.

Composing a brutal letter to the editor was followed up with a long slug of caffeine and a sense of accomplishment.

"Hey, girlfriend." Kristen plopped down in the chair across from me. She sported her usual black apron, embroidered with a swirl of steam over a coffee mug, and yellow polymer shoes. She often used my visits as an excuse to take a break.

I said, "Hey, yourself. Did you see the latest news? Tell me you didn't."

She patted my hand. "Everything's going to work out, Delaney. You'll see. People will forget about it in no time."

"Posts on the internet never go away," I reminded her.

"That newspaper guy is just doing his job. It'll blow over."

"In the meantime, I'm the talk of the town. One of the hazards of small-town living." I stared at the letter I'd written.

"I'm just glad the bear didn't attack you. It had to be divine intervention." She caught sight of my screen and did a doubletake, then she blanched and swallowed a couple of times. "You're sending that letter to Oliver Clang? The judge for the restaurant contest?"

"He's the one that posted the article, so yes, I was planning on it."

She gave me an intense look. "If you think that's what you need to do." Kristen was obviously worried about me upsetting the judge. She was my strongest and most loyal supporter and was in need of a little boost herself. Some solidarity was called for here.

"Well, now that I think about it, it probably wouldn't do any good." I hit the delete button. "But it felt good…to write it, anyway." I closed my laptop and slid it into its case.

"Delaney, you shouldn't've deleted that." She splayed a hand over her chest. "You can send a letter if you want. Can you go into your trash file and retrieve it?"

"Nah. I'm going to forget about it, like you said." I sighed and leaned my elbow on the table, cupping a hand under my chin. Daydreaming about ripping Oliver Clang a new one as soon as Kristen had her award in hand, I was brought back to the present when she cleared her throat.

"Where's your Murder Board? Why don't you go get it? Maybe that will make you feel better."

"It's upstairs."

"Go on. Bring it down."

I let out a burst of air. "All right, I will." I ran into Axle upstairs while he was on the phone. I told him to meet me downstairs when he was done with his call. I took the stairs two at a time and rushed back inside. The three of us—Kristen and Guy and me—stared at the Murder Board with crossed arms.

Kris asked, "What did McKenna do to cause someone to want to kill her? Did it have to do with the

150

music contest she won?"

I inclined my head. "Maybe. A trip to Nashville and the Grand Ole Opry."

Guy said, "That doesn't seem worth killing someone over."

I protested, "I think it might to somebody."

"Surely there's a person out there who knows something," Kris said.

Guy asked, "But where to start?"

The sound of hard boots on the painted cement floor made the three of us wheel around. Axle crossed the dining room in a few strides. "Hey, everybody." He looked past me to the Murder Board. "You've added some stuff?"

"Yeah." We all stared at the board again. "Anyone have an idea?" I asked. There were headshakes all around.

Guy said, "Delaney, you haven't even inquired about our new roasting machine."

I'm so bad, caught up in not one but two mysterious deaths. Of course my dad's death was always in the back of my mind. I did need to put at least that one aside for the time being. "Oh, sorry. Is that the one that roasts one pound at a time? How's that going, Kris?"

A smile cracked her lips open. "Great. I got some new coffee bags, too. Look." She pointed toward the shelves holding her shop's mugs, flavorings, and the soft bags of fresh roasted coffee with the shop's name on them. "My goal is to market my own brand on the internet and ship all over the world. Once I have the contest money in hand, that is."

"That's cool." Axle gave her a high five. "You going to do your own marketing?"

"To start with."

"We'd like to hire a band promotor. Someone to schedule more gigs, that is…well, we'll see." Axle frowned.

Kristen plucked at my elbow. "Follow me. I'll show you the new machine."

Guy pulled shots to make Axle a drink, while Kristen demonstrated her new roaster for me.

When her demo finished, I turned back toward the rain hitting the window, twirling the end of my braid with my fingers, thinking how everyone seemed to have plans. I really hoped things would go well for Kris's business and that Axle's band would find a new singer.

Zach pushed through the door with another man in uniform, and together they got in line. Kristen greeted them with a smile and told Guy to give them whatever they wanted without charge. She hastened to my side.

"Watch out, that's Zach's boss." Kristen indicated the other police officer with a jerk of her head. His peaked cap held more gold braid than Zach's.

"No kidding?" I tried to hide the Murder Board behind my back, but it stuck out on both sides of my body. I elbowed Axle, "Hey, let's get you to work," and edged toward the door, the board bumping the back of my legs, but Zach caught up with me, his nonfat latte in hand.

"Hi, Delaney. What's that you have there?" He had on his usual happy grin.

"Nothing." I managed to put a welcome smile on my face. "Well, I need to get going."

Kristen said, "It's nice of you to drop in, Zach," evidently trying to distract him.

"Let's see what you have." Zach reached around and

I slapped his hand away. He shook his head, his big chin flying left and right. "What are you hiding?"

"What?" I said, all little Miss Innocent.

His eyebrows drew together. "Give it up, Delaney."

Zach's boss sidled up to us, eyeing me with suspicion, and I stole a glance at Kris. She raised her hands up in the universal sign of surrender.

My eyes hit the ground. "Yeesh. Okay. Okay." I felt warm all over. Was I blushing?

The whole group seemed to be holding its breath as the officers' gazes swept over the board. Both men were red faced when they glanced back at me. I *really, really* didn't want them to know I was running my own investigation. It was the last thing I wanted…but, too late now.

"This is the police chief." Zach tossed a thumb at the other man in uniform.

"Nice to meet you." I rubbed the heel of one shoe against the other, wishing to be anywhere else.

The chief flashed a harsh look at Zach, then stuck out a finger and shook it at me. "You need to stay out of the police investigation. You could impede good police work."

I gave Kristen the *do-something!* look, but she was studying her nails. I looked to Axle but his eyes were fixed on the ceiling.

Zach said, "We'll talk about this later." Both officers turned toward the door.

I said, so only Axle and Kris could hear me, "Or, never."

Once the policemen were gone, I took a deep breath and let it out with a whoosh. "I'm sorry, Kris." It felt like I was saying that a lot lately.

"Not your fault. I was the one who told you to bring that down here." She indicated the board with a flap of her hand.

"I'll keep it upstairs from now on." I wasn't going to quit investigating McKenna's death, of course. My friends knew getting caught was not going to stop me from poking my nose into things. It hadn't before. This wasn't the first time I'd heard the lecture. I asked Kristen, "Is Zach going to be in trouble?"

"Don't worry, Delaney. You've done nothing wrong. They can't keep you from talking to people and writing things down." But Kristen's smile had slipped a bit.

Axle took the board from me. "I'll bet you uncovered something the police didn't know about. That's why they were so teed off."

"You really think so?" I said.

Guy let out a snort of disbelief. "I doubt it."

I shot him a vicious side-eye.

Kristen said, "I'll bet that's right. You found a clue they didn't. What can it be?"

She cast a few anxious glances at the door, so Guy rushed over and said, "I'll keep a lookout."

The four of us were quiet for a couple moments, thinking.

"Okay, I'll go first." I read from the board, "Victim McKenna King, age twenty-one, cause of death blunt force trauma to the head. Killed Tuesday, April 3, between 11:26 in the morning and around two in the afternoon when I spotted her car. Her fingerprints were on the steering wheel, so she drove to the scene, plus blood spatter showed she was in the driver's seat when killed."

"So, she wasn't murdered somewhere else at an earlier time and moved there," Kris pointed out.

"That's right," I agreed.

Kris asked, "What about that witness? The name I got from Zach?"

"Kabir Bhatt. I talked to him. Interesting guy, works for NOAA. He gave me these pictures." I pointed toward the photos showing the cracked snowpack.

"What do you know about McKenna?" Guy asked Axle.

"Never met her."

I said, "We know she was Kelsey's sister. We know she won the grand prize on the television show, *Rocky Mountain High Note*, with a trip to Nashville. We know she had a boyfriend who doesn't live nearby and has an alibi. What we don't know is the guy's name. Ephraim wouldn't tell me, and Kelsey didn't give me his name either."

Kristen's gaze retracted from the Murder Board back to me. "You actually know a lot about McKenna."

"But why are these people suspects?" Guy slid a finger down the list of names. "Mace, Justin, Barlow? Why would they want to hurt McKenna?"

I glanced at Axle. "Uh, I don't know…professional jealousy?"

Axle snapped, "Objection!"

"What? This isn't a court of law."

"You have no evidence, Perry Mason, so that don't fly." Axle fluttered his lips, making a rude sound. "I can see that you don't trust anyone in the band, Delaney."

"Were you able to talk to them, Axle?"

He grunted, "Not yet," and plucked the Murder Board from my grasp. "Time to head out."

Guy stopped me and hissed in my ear, "Does it make you feel important to act like the police and try to solve the crime?" My face and neck flushed warmly, and I quickened my pace out the door after Axle.

Once we were both seated in my Fiat, I said, "Guy doesn't like me."

"Why do you think that?"

"Only because it's obvious." I turned the ignition key.

He raised the Murder Board with one hand and shoved a fist against it with another, catapulting the board into the backseat.

"What did the guys think about Kelsey quitting?"

"We're still trying to figure out what to do."

I drove a couple of blocks down Fifth and left-turned into Oberly Motors. Before I'd even put the Fiat in park, Axle popped open the car door and headed for the autobody shop. I unlocked the gate to my impound space and swiveled behind the wheel of my self-loader.

Axle wasn't the only one who had to earn a living, so I traversed the city streets looking for stalled vehicles. Restless and unable to focus on work, I tumbled the clues around in my mind, but nothing else hit me. Maybe I should just stick to the car hauling business…but no, that wasn't going to happen. My mind raced. I wish I could put the woman's death behind me, but I couldn't.

There was a killer out there.

Chapter 12

I'd turned my apartment key in the lock when Kristen thrust open her door across the landing. "Hey, you two. I have something to tell you. Come in here."

Ax and I looked at each other. I'd picked him up from work and we'd just gotten home. He jerked his head toward Kris, and we both shuffled inside her place.

"The police chief gave Zach a warning." Kris was almost wringing her hands. She was dressed in a cute yellow dress, probably going out with Zach later.

"Why? What kind of warning?"

"Some of the stuff Zach told me, and I told you, was on the Murder Board. Like that guy's name, Kabir Bhatt. Zach was warned not to give out any more information or he'd be written up."

OMG!

"Go down and get that board out of the Fiat, would you, Axle?" I handed him my keys and he took off. "I'm going to lock that thing in my closet, I swear. I'm so, so sorry this happened."

With her yellow dress and fidgeting hands she looked like a nervous baby chick. She said, "Of course once the crime is solved, it'll all be forgotten. It will all work out. And you are not to feel bad, Delaney. It's not your fault."

"It *is* my fault, Kris. I shouldn't've asked you to talk

to Zach about it."

"Don't give it another thought." Her hands relaxed. "God's looking after Zach. He's watching over us."

Axle banged back through the door. "The Murder Board's on your bed, Delaney."

"Thanks, Ax." I gave him a stiff smile.

"So, Kris, you mad at that police chief?" Axle leaned in with an eager look.

"Not at all. It'll all come to nothing." She gave out a sigh and smoothed down her hair, back to her calm and serene self. That nervous chick had flown the coop.

Axle said to me, "See, she never gets mad. Didn't I tell you that?"

My eyes went back to my best friend. I wondered what it would be like to be so confident that everything was going to turn out. I said to Kris, "You're perfect. It's not fair."

She laughed. "No, I'm not. And I could use a group hug."

Axle, who normally ran from such things, wrapped his arms around both of us and we intertwined our arms with his. But not for long. After half a sec, he jumped back.

"I'd be willing to smack that police chief around." He was sturdy and slightly intimidating in his baggy pants and sweatshirt with a skull and crossbones. He put up his fists and mock punched the air, then his gestures turned into a drum routine.

"Funny, Axle. You know I love you?" Kristen laughed.

Axle met her words with an eye roll, but I could tell he was pleased that Kris laughed. We left Kris to finish getting ready for her date.

Upon entering our apartment, I chucked my purse on the counter and snapped Boss's leash to his collar. Axle and I returned down the stairs. When we stepped onto the pavement, Boss stretched up his muzzle and sniffed the air. At a break in traffic, we ran across the busy street and I let the retractable leash out so Boss could frisk around. I held the cord tight while the *Rottie* buried his nose in the bushes and lifted a leg at the foot of the bench. Once he finished his sniffing inspection, I said, "Good baby, good puppy," in my best puppy talk, and we made our way back home.

As I hung Boss's leash on the hook, Axle hunched over the open refrigerator, then slammed it shut. "Let's order pizza."

"Sounds great. Call it in." I was glad this teen was hungry. That had to be a good sign that he was getting over Kelsey's departure from the band. I scooted down the hall to bury the Murder Board deep inside my closet. I backtracked to the kitchen, hitched my bottom onto the counter stool, and stretched out my high-heeled feet. "I almost forgot. Kelsey sent her sister a text…"

"So what?" He rubbed the back of his neck. "Everybody texts."

"I saw it on her phone and took a picture of it. I haven't even read it yet."

His eyes widened and he made a *gimme* gesture. "Hand it over."

"So you don't mind that I snooped around after all."

He snatched my phone away from me. I gripped Axle's arm as our gazes went over the words, and when I finished first, my eyes followed his progress down the screen.

This is what it said:

How could U steal my boyfriend AND the songs I wrote? One is bad enuf, but U stole everything I care about. It doesn't matter that U won an award WITH MY SONGS, what matters most is that my sister, whom I trusted, would do such a thing to me. I'LL NEVER FORGIVE U.

I asked, "What do you think, Axle?"

"Wow, I don't know." He peeled my hand off his arm.

"Kelsey has a motive." I gave him my best I-told-you-so pop of the eyes and he slightly nodded. "So, you agree with me then?" I fist-bumped his shoulder.

He rocked away, then back. "Why didn't she delete the text? I would've if I was the killer."

"Crafty, crafty. You think like a killer. But can't the police recover deleted texts from the service provider? I saw that on TV."

"You're right, if they haven't been overwritten yet."

"I'm right? Did you just say I'm right? Are you okay?" I teased, but Axle pretended he didn't hear me. I asked, "Did Kelsey really write her own songs? That takes some skill to be able to sing and compose, too."

"She did. A lot of artists write their own tunes." His face puckered. "Another thing the band's going to miss."

We looked at each other, shaking our heads.

The bell rang. Axle shot off the stool and raced Boss to the door. "Pizza's here."

I grabbed Boss's collar to keep him from bolting when Axle swung open the door. Standing behind the delivery guy were Mace and Justin. Axle accepted the two large pizza boxes from the driver and ushered his fellow band members inside.

"What's this?" I asked.

Axle explained, "I told the band to come over so you can talk to them, see for yourself they couldn't've had anything to do with McKenna's death. None of us did, including Kelsey. That's why I ordered the extra pizza."

Justin shed his coat. "We had nowhere else to go since the gig was cancelled for tonight. We had nowhere else to be." Disappointment was written on his face.

"Thank you for coming." I put a little sarcasm in my voice.

While they threw their coats on the living room sofa, I went to the cupboard for plates. The aroma of pepperoni, cheese, and grease hit my nose and made my mouth water, and Boss had drool hanging from his lips. Axle brought cans of light beer to the table.

I asked the other band members, "You all old enough to drink?"

Mace said, "Of course, man," and Axle gave me a look of horror. Axle wasn't yet twenty-one, but the others did appear older.

"Taking your word for it," I said, passing out napkins.

Once we had the gooey slices on plates, including one on the floor for Boss, Axle told me, "We're not sure what we're going to do without Kelsey."

"I'm sorry this happened. I wish I could help. I mean, help in any way other than lip syncing."

They all nodded, mouths full.

Axle said, "So, Delaney, ask your questions."

I looked at the guitar player with the long hair and brooding eyes. "So, you first, Mace. Where were you Tuesday, April third? Between 11:26 in the morning and around two in the afternoon?" A string of cheese stuck to my pizza and I had to stretch it out to bite it off.

"I was home all day by myself till we met up at Roasters around four. Is that the time McKenna was killed?"

"Yes."

"Well, actually, I had a package delivered at 12:30 or so." He tapped into his phone, then twirled it around for everyone to see. "Here's my doorbell video recording. See me meeting the delivery guy at the door and signing for the package?"

"Oh, yeah." I nodded after checking the time stamp on the video.

"It takes a couple hours to get to the top of Clarkson Pass from my house. No way I could've driven there in time, especially with the snowstorm up there."

"Okay, that makes sense. How about you, Justin?"

"I was at the library in town studying. I've got exams coming up. My study group can vouch for me from noon to three-thirty when I left for Roasters. But I don't know why I need an alibi. I didn't know Kelsey's sister."

Axle threw down a wadded-up napkin. "Neither of you knew McKenna, right?"

The two shook their heads in almost perfect unison.

"Never met her once?" I asked.

They shook their heads again.

Axle pointed to himself. "Me either." He drummed his first two fingers on the edge of the counter.

I asked, "Do any of you know who Kelsey was going out with? They might have broken up recently." She had accused her sister of stealing her boyfriend in the text message I'd shown Axle.

"Kelsey?" Justin drew out the word, as if thinking long and hard.

"There's something you know?" I pressed.

"Spit it out, man." Axle jabbed his finger at his friend.

"I know a guy ditched her, and Kelsey was cut deep. I got the impression he took up with another singer."

Axle and I locked glances. He said, "I know it looks bad, especially with what you found, Delaney."

I gave Axle the *keep-quiet* stare, hoping he wouldn't bring up Kelsey's text. I might get in trouble for looking at her phone if anyone found out. But the other singer Kelsey's boyfriend took up with *was* probably McKenna. I turned back to the other two. "Anything else you can think of?"

Mace whipped back his long hair. "Like what?"

"Did Kelsey have any enemies? I know I'm grasping at straws," I admitted, "but if she did, maybe that person disliked her sister, too."

Mace looked thoughtful, but didn't say anything.

I said, "Anything odd? Unusual? No matter how small it seems."

Justin's face became animated. "I know. Kelsey was worried about Barlow. She's a bit afraid of the guy because her sister had a stalker. She told me that."

"That's important." I cut my eyes to Justin. "And you at least knew Kelsey had a sister."

"I never met her, like I said, and I didn't know her name. I only knew *about* her. And that she had a stalker."

I planted my hands on my hips. "You should've led with this."

Axle said, "See, we're being helpful."

"But no idea who the stalker was?" I asked.

Justin shook his head. I wondered how I could find out about him, and whether I should simply ask Kelsey.

The guys kept up an excited chatter while I loaded the dinner dishes into the dishwasher. They retreated to the couches, feet up on the coffee table, talking about whether they should cancel the rest of their scheduled events. I slipped down the hall and pulled the Murder Board out of my closet. I crossed out Justin's and Mace's names. They both had alibis and neither had a motive.

Then I wrote in red, *stalker*.

And underlined the word twice.

Soon I heard epic music and the sounds of gunfire and explosions. So, while the guys played video games, I stayed in my room with my laptop. First, I went on the prison website to request another meeting with Rob Abington. Why not? I had no other leads into my dad's death and what could Rob do to me? I wasn't afraid of him. Then I switched gears and queried *McKenna King, award-winning musician, and Rocky Mountain High Note*. There were quite a few posts about the hit television program, which I mostly clicked through, but one item buried on page three caught my eye. An article posted by Oliver Clang in the Spruce Ridge online newspaper.

There I learned about McKenna's ability to hit the E7 high note. Not many achieved her vocal range. The article was well written and complimentary, portraying McKenna in a favorable light. There were hundreds of comments, so it was well read, too, and it didn't even contain any conspiracy theories.

My cheeks burned as I thought about the bear article showing me in a not-so-favorable light. Why do I get the ridicule and McKenna the praise? Maybe because she deserved the raves and I didn't. I had a pain in my stomach that was probably envy, but I was not admitting that out loud.

If Kelsey was jealous of her sister, I could understand that. I was a little bit envious myself. Did McKenna win as a result of Kelsey's original songs combined with McKenna's own incredible singing ability? And how did Kelsey feel about it?

I typed McKenna's name and the word, *obituary*, in the query box and found the funeral notice. Next of kin included her parents, one sister, aunts, uncles, and cousins. Her awards were listed all the way back to high school. An early morning funeral mass was to take place at the Catholic church with a graveside ceremony right afterwards.

Kelsey hadn't said anything to us about a funeral, but then I hadn't asked. So much for being thorough. It was a good idea I remembered to check now, because the service was tomorrow.

****

I skipped McKenna's funeral mass, but showed up for the graveside ceremony at Mountain View Cemetery, the only burial place in town. A long green lawn provided an unobstructed view of flat grave markers and the occasional tall tombstone. Poking out of the ground here and there were miniature American flags fluttering in the wind. The parking lot held the typical rows of SUVs, mostly in dark colors. A few white. A few blue. All with little black bows on the antennas.

A middle-aged couple, red-eyed and clutching tissues, emerged from a long limo, and the priest and Kelsey exited next. Other mourners popped out of their parked cars and marched uneasily after the family over to an awning that shaded recently turned earth. Buttoning my jacket against the wind, I joined the crowd at the gravesite. The loamy smell of spring with a slight floral scent was on the early morning breeze. Two chairs provided seating for Mom and Dad. Everyone else stood while the casket on a tall cart was rolled into place.

The priest, wearing a black robe with white vestments over his shoulders, spoke for about ten minutes, ending with something like *requiem* and other words in Latin. Kelsey sang "Wind Beneath my Wings" a cappella, her high voice sweet and true. Then she helped her parents back to the limo while the crowd broke apart to return to their cars.

A man stood next to the grave, and suddenly realizing he was Oliver Clang without his orange sneakers, I lingered around, too. The last car door shut with a thud and Clang lit up a cigarette.

I walked up to him. "Are you going to write another article about McKenna? The one you wrote about her already was nice."

He sucked smoke into his lungs on a gasp and barked out a cough. "What are you doing here?"

"My roommate is in a band with her sister, Kelsey. *Was* in a band with Kelsey. *Is* in a band that Kelsey *was*…" I gave up. "I'm here to pay my respects."

"I've done my homework. I know about you. You think you're some kind of amateur sleuth, but you only get in the way of the police. Are you trying to obfuscate the investigation? And why? Is there something you don't want anyone to discover? Or do you have a wild idea about who did it?" He brought out a small notepad and stubby pencil.

My head whipped around so fast I nearly fell off my heels. "I suppose you're going to print that crazy theory?"

"What have you found out? I might print that. Tell me." His hands gripped the pad and pencil, his cigarette stuck to his lips.

I ducked my head. "No comment."

"That's what they all say." He tossed his cigarette butt into the open pit. Disrespectful, *amiright?*

The wind caught our pant legs causing them to flap, and the miniature flags rippled in rows along the graves. "How's the contest judging going?" I asked.

He shoved his notebook into his pocket. "It's winding down, thankfully. I'm so tired of dropping into restaurants, checking out their restrooms, trying everything on the menu."

"You do all that?"

"Yeah. Then we have to fill out a form. It has questions about the staff, cleanliness, menu options, all kinds of questions. It takes a lot of time." He stared into the sky. "I wonder where all that information goes, ultimately? Into some kind of huge database?"

I shrugged. "Do you know who the mystery judge is?"

"None of the judges know who the fourth one is. We'll find out when everyone else does. Why all the secrecy, I don't know. It's as if they're plotting something, like they can control the outcome by using a mystery judge. It's not being transparent."

I nodded as if in agreement.

He continued on. "I thought judging the contest would bring in advertisements, or at least more subscriptions, but that's not happening. I probably won't volunteer again."

"You mean restaurants buy ads to get your vote?" Would Kristen go for that if I suggested it?

"No, no, not at all. But, hey, I've got to get the newspaper's name out there somehow. It's a dying business. The internet will be the downfall of the newspaper industry. It's part of the plan. It's all about control."

"So you understand how hard marketing is when you have a small business. That's why I complained when you posted that bear article."

He wore a satisfied smirk. "By the way, thank you. Those videos on the paper's news site have thousands of views. You got some publicity out of it, and so did I. Just check the comments. You can quit your complaining."

"Really?" I thumbed the site open on my phone. The bear video had over twenty thousand views. The clip rolled over automatically to play the next video, the one of me with the Tesla.

His sneer fell into a deep frown and his eyebrows pinched together with a knob of skin nudged out between them. "McKenna was a complainer, too. She wanted me to print her press releases verbatim. I'm a newspaperman, not her publicist."

"You gave her a good write-up. How could she complain about that?"

"I agree, but she wanted more, the spoiled brat. What a diva." He pivoted on his heel. "I'm out of here."

He jumped into his Chevy Silverado, a four-wheel drive pickup with a blade, and melted snow flew up from the wheels as he accelerated out of the lot.

Chapter 13

Although I knew I was torturing myself, I opened Spruce Ridge's online news site on my phone and scrolled through the comments.

The posts under the bear video were for the most part favorable. People were amazed. They were awed. They were entertained.

I was relieved.

But the other article about me spotting a dead woman on Clarkson Pass included a recent comment with the question, "Why would a tow truck driver investigate a murder?" A snapshot of my Murder Board was attached to the post. Only it was the earlier version with my crude stick figure and cartoonish drawing of the car, making the board look as amateurish and ridiculous as possible.

The first idea that came to mind was that one of my friends leaked the photo to the news editor, but rational thought took over. None of them would turn on me like that. When the Murder Board was in Kris's office, it's possible someone could've sneaked in and taken the photo. And Guy, not a fan of mine, was highest on the possibility scale, but to be fair, it could've been anyone. I set my phone aside.

It was late morning now. My truck and I chugged out of town up the canyon where the pines scented the air. Flicking the indicator, I rolled the truck to a stop at a rest area off I-70. If any highway accidents were reported over the on-dash police scanner, I was positioned to be the first to arrive.

After playing solitaire for ten minutes, I was already bored. Bored and frustrated, both destructive feelings. I wouldn't be playing so much solitaire if Axle was with me. I almost called him, but I called Mom instead.

She told me all about her new neighbors who'd moved in a week ago down the street. Don't ask how she had the intel so fast. After she asked how I was, I launched into a tirade about the news editor-slash-contest judge, without mentioning my investigation or the Murder Board. Some things are best left unsaid. Besides, he started it. None of this would've made it on the internet if it hadn't been for him. I ended with, "The only reason the guy volunteered to be a judge is to get more subscribers and advertisers for his online news site. Can you believe it?"

"That's called networking, Laney."

I let out a little sigh. I hated him.

Mom said, "I wish there was something I could do to give Kristen an edge. What if I put up posters around Spruce Ridge that say Roasters is the best coffee shop in town? A-number one."

"Mom, this isn't glee club. I was hoping the band could keep playing at Roasters to bring in more people, and if any of the judges showed up, they'd see a full coffee shop of happy customers, but they aren't playing anymore. The lead female singer quit."

She cleared her throat. "I could fill in and sing for the band."

Stifling a scream at the back of my throat, I said,

"That's sweet, but they need someone full time." I rubbed my eyes to free myself from the image of videos headlined, *Mother of high-heeled tow truck driver singing sensation.* "Any other ideas besides that?"

"I could post some nice comments on social media."

"You never post or comment. You're a lurker—" I stopped myself. "You know, Mom, that would be a nice thing to do. Why don't you do that?"

Once we disconnected, I watched traffic on I-70 for a while and listened to the loud grind of the diesel engines. Before too long, I gave up waiting there and drove back into town. After steering down Main Street, I took a random right and coasted past a row of two-stories with wide front porches. I recognized the white house with black shutters and Barlow's Chrysler PT Cruiser, front-wheel drive, pulling into the driveway.

Barlow got out and waved at me. "Hey, Delaney."

I pulled over to the curb and powered down my window. "Hello, Barlow. Are you waving me down? You having car trouble? Can't be your ignition switch."

"No, that's fixed. The car's fine." He walked up to my driver's window. "How are you doing? Doesn't look like you're busy."

"I'm working." I chewed the inside of my cheek. "I have a question for you. Did you know Kelsey's sister had a stalker?" I studied his face.

His nostrils widened. "No! Who was it?"

"I don't know. I thought you might." It takes one to know one, right?

His eyes narrowed, then he shook his head. "I have no idea. Remember, I told you I didn't know McKenna."

"Then how did you know she won the singing competition?"

He leaned into my window, and I pushed back against my seat. With the window rolled down the dry scent of pine blew in.

His face looked deep in thought. "Let's see…I was over at Main Street Brewery. All the televisions are usually tuned to sports, but there was this reality show on one of the screens, *Rocky Mountain High Note*, and it happened to be the season finale where they announced the winner."

"You seem to be everywhere, Barlow." I'd run into him at the wine tasting room, at the bagel place, I don't know how many times at the coffee shop, and anywhere the band was playing. Talk about *creepish*. Of course, he could be wondering why I was driving down his street, I supposed. Only, it's my job.

He took a second to respond. "I eat out a lot."

"Oh." That could explain it. Probably a single guy without much of a life.

I checked the time on the dash. "I'd better get going. Goodbye, Barlow." I cranked the engine and he took the hint by retreating a few steps. I circled the truck back to Main and patrolled the towaway zones until the time came when I could go home.

****

The phone woke me from sleep, so I answered, drowsy and disoriented. I did that half asleep-half awake driving maneuver to pick up my tow truck and arrived at the vehicle break-down in twenty minutes. A Jeep Patriot, front-wheel drive, was on the side of the road with a buckled front hood and one flat tire.

The man standing by the Jeep said, "So, you're a tow truck driver," and laughed. "Sorry. I've never met a female tow truck driver before."

172

I gave him a tight grin, glad I hadn't shown up in high heels. It was too late at night, and I was too tired. He was lucky I'd shown up at all. I was cognizant enough to ask, "What happened? It looks like an accident? Your front end's damaged."

A muscle jumped in the man's cheek. "No, that dent was already there, but it's probably the reason the engine conked out. Then the flat happened. I must've had a slow leak." I gave the area around us a quick study. No other cars were in sight, but it was dark with the moon hidden behind cloud cover.

Should I call the police anyway? This wreck looked suspicious. Something didn't feel right.

"Can we get going?" He glanced at his watch. "It's two in the morning."

I didn't want to wake Zach. I was enough of a blister on Zach's bunions already. It would take a headless zombie driving a flying vehicle for me to call Zach. Maybe I should alert 9-1-1, but there was no real emergency. The guy didn't appear injured, just foolish for attempting to drive a car in this condition.

"Okay." I punched the button on the wireless remote that operated the T-bar and lowered the claws to the ground. I dragged a sleeve over the wheel-lift arm to elevate the flattened tire so the car would rise evenly. Then I hit another button. The claws snagged the front tires and the boom elevated the Jeep. After strapping the wheels and affixing the LED tow lights, I told my customer to get in the truck. Once he was buckled in, I captured the Jeep's VIN on my cell phone camera. I deposited him and his Jeep at his house and took his money. He actually had two hundred in cash on him.

Sleep claimed me as soon as I hit the pillow, but all

too soon my vibrating phone danced on the bedside table jarring me back awake.

"Why didn't you call the police?"

"Zach?"

"Yes." It sounded as if he spit out the word like the bad taste of coffee with curdled milk.

I pried my eyes open. "What?"

"You towed a Jeep Patriot."

"Yes."

"Are you capable of saying more than one word?"

"No." Because I was sleep deprived. "What time is it?"

"Six. That driver did thousands of dollars of damage to a legally parked car. We're going to have to charge you for moving his vehicle after the fact."

I elbowed myself to a sitting position. "I asked him if he'd been in an accident. He lied to me. And I never saw a second car."

"The impact forced the other car into the ditch."

"It was too dark to see." I drubbed a fist to my forehead. "So, all those times when you got mad that I called, and you told me not to phone, not to bother the police, this time I should've just ignored everything you said before?"

"Delaney, you contaminated a crime scene."

"Not on purpose. And how did I mess it up exactly? You can still prosecute him, right? I'll give you a sworn statement."

"Come in to the station later today." There was a click and the connection went dead. I swung my legs over the side of the bed to sit up.

Contaminating a crime scene was what I was trying *not* to do when I left McKenna's Subaru Legacy undisturbed on Clarkson Pass. Not exactly intentional because I didn't know then it was a crime scene, but all the same...I hadn't interfered then, as Zach would say.

No one thanked me for that. In fact, I felt a bit shamed by the whole experience.

I ripped through my shower, dressed in a sweater and jeans, stuffed my feet into heels, and applied shiny lip balm. Staring into the mirror, I decided more was necessary and gobbed on eyeliner and mascara. I'd just hiked my purse onto my shoulder when a brisk knock sounded at the door.

When I let him in, Ephraim perused me from head to toe. "You're looking beautiful today, Delaney."

"Thanks, Ephraim." I blushed under his scrutiny. "Why'd you stop by?"

"I'm on my way into the station." He took a deep breath, stretching his uniform across his muscled chest. "You saw the news?"

"No." I bristled, certain it wasn't good. The day started off bad. Could it get any worse? No, just no. "More news? What is it this time?"

"Nothing to worry about. In fact, don't even read it. Just ignore it because nothing will come of it." He ran a hand down my back. "I have to get going. You'll be okay?"

"Yes." Fat chance of that.

"Okay, then. I'll call you later."

As soon as he was out the door, I ran for my computer to check the online news. When I was done, I wanted to smash something. I'm sure you can guess what it was about.

Tow truck driver known for high-heeled antics taints evidence.

Written by Oliver Clang, of course.

Not only my name was mentioned, but there was an unflattering statement about my red hair and my shoes. And that I reported an allegedly dead woman but not an auto accident. No mention that the dead woman report was true.

Why was Oliver Clang so mean to me? What did I ever do to him? This was probably an indication that Kristen was knocked out of the competition. And what did Ephraim mean that nothing will come of it? Was he going to talk to Zach and demand I not be charged? If he didn't, Kristen would, and I got some satisfaction from that, but resentment surged through me anyway.

I needed my li'l cuz to weigh in, so I stormed down the short hall to Axle's bedroom and threw open the door, banging it against the wall. Boss exploded into barking, realized it was me, then hopped off the bed and galloped toward me. He jumped on my knees.

"I'm excited to see you, too. Do you love me? Do you love me? I love you." I made kissy sounds and my blood pressure went down several notches.

Axle cracked one eye open. "You need me for a tow?"

"No."

He glanced toward the window, but the closed shades kept the room dark. "What time is it?"

"It's seven. Sun's up."

He rolled onto his side, so I tottered over in my heels and perched my butt on the edge of his bed. He poked his head out from under his pillow. "All right. What's the glitch?"

"Last night I towed a Jeep Patriot from an accident scene without calling the police first." I twisted toward him and held both palms up. "I saw the damage but not the other car, and the guy lied to me. He said he hadn't been in an accident."

"So, what's the big *fricking* deal?"

"I know, right? But I guess it's a crime. Zach threatened to charge me with contaminating the scene, and it made the Spruce Ridge news."

He sat up and the covers fell away. He'd slept in his clothes like he always did, and his T-shirt with a band's name, Badflower, looked like it needed a turn in the washing machine. "That's not cool."

"So true." I pounded a fist on the bed covers.

"Is the coffee made?" He stifled a yawn.

"I'll go start it." I split for the kitchen to fill the coffee maker.

Boss trotted to the door and scratched on it, so while the coffee brewed, I leashed him up and took him across the street to the park.

"I can't let you off leash, Boss. Not since you turned into a runaway."

He lashed his tongue against my hand to let me know he understood. Maintaining a death grip on Boss, I sank onto the bench with my legs extended and tipped my head back.

A horn blared from busy Pine Street, and I didn't even flinch, but when someone yelled, "Hey you! Stilettos kick ass!" I bolted upright. Two teens I didn't recognize in a Dodge Charger, rear-wheel drive, waved their arms out the windows and sped off.

I glanced at my footwear. Red stilettos, bright red to match my angry mood, and yes, the shoes were *kickin'*. But those words were strikingly similar to the graffiti painted on Roasters a week ago and even similar to the news article today. I shot off the bench and ran tippy-toe on my high heels for Roasters. With Boss racing ahead, I rounded the corner and slowed down.

The building had not been tagged.

I bent double, shaking and out of breath, but relieved.

Back inside the apartment, I scooped dog kibble into Boss's bowl, and while the *Rottie* crunched, I poured myself a steaming cup of coffee. Following the aroma, Axle appeared, went for the cabinet, then up to me with an empty cup held straight out.

As I poured the liquid energy, I told him what just happened. He offered me an awkward but comforting shoulder squeeze. "That news guy sure has it out for you."

"I'm afraid to show my face outside," I admitted. Teens had already shouted at me from a passing car.

His head fell on his chest as he studied the floor. "Byron needs me today or I'd ride along with you."

"Okay." I puffed out my cheeks.

"I know what you should do," he said with a grin. "Wear a disguise."

I snorted a laugh.

"Why not? Cover that red hair." He patted my head, hard. "Ditch the heels, just for today." He pointed to my shoes. "Put on dark shades." He gestured like he was sliding glasses over his nose. "No one will know it's you. Go incognito."

"Hard to pass up, but no."

He rapped a bony knuckle on the top of my head. "Come on, it's a good idea. Give me some credit for thinking of it."

"Ow! That hurt, you twerp." But I was actually

starting to warm to his suggestion. "Do you have an extra beanie? One that's clean?"

He dashed over to the laundry basket and rifled through a pile of clothes. He handed me a beanie. "Right here."

I made the eeew-gross face. "Out of the dirty laundry? You call that clean?"

"Take it." He waved the hat. "It's from the clean laundry basket. I haven't put my stuff away yet."

I splayed my hand across my chest. "You? You did laundry?"

"Funny." He yanked the knit cap down over the top of my head, then circled me as he stuffed my hair underneath the edge of the cap. I sniffed the air, but didn't smell any stink so maybe Axle had done the laundry. "Do you have big sunglasses?" he asked.

I gave him a thumbs up. "From the Jackie O collection."

Chapter 14

I slunk down the apartment stairs in my Axle-inspired ensemble—beanie, dark glasses, hoodie, baggy jeans, and black Chucks. In other words, I looked like him but in Jackie O sunglasses.

Spruce Ridge's police station sat on the corner of Main Street in an old brick one-story with black and white police cruisers lined up at the door. Visitors occupied orange plastic chairs in the low budget lobby decorated with fake ficus trees, black scuffed linoleum, and photos of stern-faced chiefs of police for the last fifty years.

When I asked for Zach Bowers, the duty clerk conducted me through the security door into the bullpen. The halls were sterile. The noise of ringing phones and everyone clickity-clacking away at their keyboards was stentorian. The clerk whisked me past Zach's gray iron desk—he kept his head down, not meeting my eyes—and into a small interrogation room.

I was sitting there thinking, *now what?*

The two-way mirror reflected my image. I hardly recognized that lumpy head from the thick hair tucked under the cap. The disguise worked.

An officer I didn't know entered the room. "Please take off your sunglasses."

I complied. I still hardly recognized myself in the

mirror because of the extra eye make-up I had on today. I'd forgotten about that.

"Fill out this statement." He handed me a form and a pen.

"Are you going to charge me?"

"No. All we need is a statement."

"Thank you." I filled in the paper, emphasizing the lies told by my customer. Feeling slightly like a police informant, I added the VIN I'd recorded on my phone along with the driver's description. I signed my name and handed the statement to the officer.

On my way back through the bullpen, I searched out Zach, but he kept his face pointed away. He was avoiding me just like I was avoiding everybody else today.

My phone buzzed with an email in my inbox, so I read it while unlocking my Fiat. My request for another inmate visit was denied. The form email had the following reason checkmarked: *inmate refused meeting.* So Rob didn't want to see me. That line of inquiry was a closed door.

I drove over to Oberly Motors to pick up my tow truck, and when I arrived, Byron came out to meet me at the gate.

"Axle's here. He tole me all about your trouble with the police." Byron rubbed a red rag down his face and poked it into his overall pocket.

"Hello to you, too, Old Man." I punched in the code to unlock the secured area. "Let me get my truck, and I'll come inside so we can talk."

"One of Axle's friends stopped by. Justin. They're in there now."

I scrunched my forehead. "Okay."

He sauntered back toward the garage doors, and I

exchanged my Fiat for the truck, then left the truck parked out front.

When I entered the lobby, Byron's questioning gaze made my hands fidgety. "Don't worry, Ol' Man, it's not like I'm going to be arrested or anything." I nodded a hello at Justin slouching next to Axle on the brown couch.

"I was more worried about ya goin' ballistic," Byron said, smoothing back what was left of his hair.

"Can't guarantee anything," I joked, then said, "The police only wanted my statement. They didn't charge me after all."

He gave me a smile and appeared to relax. "Tell her what happened, Ax. Now go on."

"What is it?" I noticed Axle's frown. His mouth puckered and his eyes went to the ceiling. Was it something *I* did? What could I have done now? My mind traveled in so many different directions. "Are you upset with me?"

"Nothing you did, for once." Axle hunched his shoulders up to his ears and took a deep breath. His gaze darted to Justin who wore the trace of a scowl. "The band's calling it quits. It's over. We're going our separate ways..." Axle trailed off, looking into his lap with an anguished expression.

"Oh, man, I'm so sorry. But, why? Why break up the band?" I alternated my gaze between Axle and Justin.

Justin said, "Kelsey's moving to L.A. with some music promoter. If the talent agent saw us now without our lead singer, we'd never break into music. We're screwed."

I countered, "No, you're not. You can continue without her. Just find another singer."

Axle said, "She was special. We all agreed we'd never find anyone like her."

"There are other gifted vocalists out there. Don't give up." The guys probably had their hearts crushed, but they would eventually find someone else if they kept looking. "Am I right, Ol' Man?"

"Sure, sure. It's not the end o' the world," Byron said, but the younger men's faces were both set in gloom.

I wanted to throw in another objection but couldn't think of one.

Justin jiggled some change in his pocket. "I'm going to get a soda out of the machine. Anyone else want one?"

The rest of us shook our heads. He slogged out the door and cut across the pavement to the soda machine at the end of the last auto bay. His cell phone sat on the table and I picked it up.

"No worries. He's coming back for that," Axle said.

"Keep a lookout. Tell me when you see him get close." I flicked my finger over the screen.

Axle gripped the edge of the table. "What are you doing?"

"I'm not sure."

"Well, that's obvious. Put that down."

"Hey, it worked out the last time I snooped on someone's phone." I swiped my finger to the right.

"You still tryin' to investigate?" Byron asked.

"Why not?" When I wasn't breaking the law one way, I was breaking it another way. I was restless and antsy. Even solitaire didn't keep me occupied anymore. And crime solving took my mind off my troubles. I found the icon for the camera and tapped on that. My fingers ripped through the pictures until I got to a jaw-dropper.

I put a hand over my mouth. *Yowzah!*

"Delaney, your eyes are popping out. What is it?" Byron asked.

I lifted a palm, like *hold on a sec*, but Axle grabbed the phone out of my hands.

Justin stepped through the door and we all jumped. "What's going on?"

Heat flooded my cheeks and my pulse spiked. Axle tossed him his phone and he caught it. "Don't forget your phone, man."

"Thanks." Justin took a swig of cola. "What'd I miss?"

Axle ran a hand over his brow where sweat beaded on his forehead. "We were just talking about Kristen. None of the judges have been in the coffee shop for a long time."

Axle's words surprised me. I could hardly believe he was that quick on the uptake. I said, "That's right. That's what we were talking about."

Byron stared at me with nervous twitches around his eyes.

Justin said, "The contest doesn't end for another week. There's still time." He turned to Axle. "I guess I need to go pick up my amps."

"Yeah, I need to find another place to store my drum kit." Axle rubbed a fist into his chest like he needed an antacid.

They talked about the gigs they would have to cancel, and I listened quietly, then Justin brought up again, "Too bad about Kels."

"Yeah." Axle looked as deflated as a punctured tire. He was only eighteen and still suffered from the teenager-in-love syndrome. How many times had he checked himself into heartbreak hotel? I wished there was something I could do for him.

The phone rang and Byron picked it up. "Oberly Motors. How may I help you?"

"Can I talk to you, Axle?" I waved my li'l cuz into the first auto bay. He followed me and I closed the door behind us, shutting us apart from the others.

"That was a *friggin'* nightmare," he said in a snit. "What'd you think you were doing with Justin's phone?"

"I'm trying to solve a crime, here." I folded my arms and leveled my gaze at him, but couldn't work up a decent glare.

"Not buying it. You're just nosy." He cuffed me upside the head causing my—or rather his—knit cap to fly off.

I made a wafting motion. "That's not what I wanted to talk to you about." I took hold of both of his elbows and gave him a little shake. "You need to snap out of this funk you're in, Axle. You have your whole life ahead of you. You're a gifted drummer. You are going to break into the music industry soon, I just know it."

His angry expression changed to one of laughter. He snort-laughed, then screwed up his eyes and another long laugh burst out of him.

"What?" The conversation was not going the way I thought it would.

"How old are you, Delaney?"

"What?" I repeated.

He said, "You sound *sooo* old. You're headed straight to *Oldsville*."

We both laughed, but he laughed louder, flailing his arms around. He choked on another laugh, and I thumped his back. "It's not that funny."

"Oh yes, it is." He collapsed against the wall.

"Okay, okay, *jeez*. So what? I'm older than you. And I'm going to make an adult out of you yet." The words coming out of my mouth did sound like my mother's, triggering my gag reflex.

He was biting his lips to keep from laughing some more. "See you later." He snatched his beanie off the ground and took it inside with him to rejoin Justin and Byron.

I hurried away with my head down and locked myself in my truck cab. Then I leaned back, crossed my arms, and twitched a grin. I'd just uncovered a major clue. Justin had a picture of McKenna on his phone. How could I be sure it was her and not her look-alike sister? Because the picture was of both McKenna and Kelsey singing together.

He'd denied knowing McKenna.

This proved he was lying.

But why?

Free of Axle's beanie, I scratched my head all over, then ran my fingers through my hair to comb out the long strands. Next, I gathered my hair into three bunches and threaded the strands over and under into my usual plait. I felt defeated wearing an outfit Axle picked out as a disguise. Like I couldn't wear my high heels on tows anymore. Like I couldn't be myself anymore. At least I wasn't wearing the beanie. I roared the truck to life and headed home.

Charging up my apartment steps, I unlocked the door and ran flat out to my room. I sat on the edge of my bed and pulled off my Chucks, then stripped, threw my clothes in the laundry basket, and hopped in the shower. I scrubbed my face, my makeup running down the drain.

A few minutes later I stepped out and pressed a towel against the wet strands of my curly hair, glad to be rid of the hat hair I'd come home with. While my locks air-dried, I dressed to get ready to look for stalls.

But a knock sounded before I could go out, so I answered the door. "Mom? What are you doing here?"

She stepped inside and pulled me into a hug. "I just came from seeing Nancy."

I let go of her. "What did you talk about?"

"You." She set her ginormous handbag on the counter. "I drove up here to surprise Nancy and smooth things over. I thought that was the best thing I could do to help Kristen with her contest."

"What happened?"

"All I said was, I hoped Kristen was doing well in the contest, you know, trying to see where Kris stood." Her face was a mask of hurt. "Nancy gave me quite a chilly reception."

"What did she say exactly?"

"That she didn't have time to chat."

I hugged my mom again. "It's okay. You tried. You probably just caught her at a bad moment."

"You're right. I only stopped by to let you know." She snatched her handbag and hitched it onto her shoulder. "I'm heading to the mall to pick up a few things. Do you want to come with?"

"I need to work today, Mom, but thanks for asking."

We visited for a few more minutes, promising each other to make plans soon, and then she left.

After grabbing my things, I hustled to my truck, but noticed Mace's rusty VW van parked in Roaster's lot, so instead of taking off, I entered the coffee shop. Mace was in the corner of the dining area winding up electrical cords and stuffing them into a bin next to a stack of amplifiers on a dolly.

Nancy was being a pain, Justin was a liar…but what about Mace? Was he up to something, too? Now would be a good time to find out.

I walked up to him. "Good morning, Mace. I heard the band's breaking up. I'm so sorry."

He smoothed his long hair back with both hands. "Yeah. I'm still hoping it's not over."

"Me, too."

Guy called out from the counter, "Your usual, Delaney?"

"That'd be great, Guy." I leaned a little closer to Mace so that I couldn't be overheard. "What's going on with Kelsey? Why would she leave the band high and dry like that? I suppose she's still grieving for her sister?"

"That's probably it."

That and she's a self-centered jerk, but I didn't say that out loud. "What are you going to do, Mace? Axle said you're between jobs?"

"I'm a ski instructor in the winter. I also work on cars. Maybe I'll try to finish fixing up my van, or I might need to find else something to tide me over." He lifted a heavy amplifier onto a cart and fed wires into a plastic bin.

"You used to work at L&B Garage?"

"Oh, sure, but I won't go back there." His eyes darted around the room. "Well, I'd better get this done. If I am going to work on my van, I'll need to find someplace else to store the equipment." He snapped the lid on the bin, hefted it into his arms, and started for the door.

I said, backing up my steps, "Hope to see you around, Mace," then went to the pickup counter for my coffee to-go.

Five minutes later, I drove to Main Street while the sky dripped with rain. The inside of the truck was stuffy with the scent of my new leather pumps—green for spring—mingling with the truck's ever present smell of motor oil.

As I glided past tourist shops, expensive boutiques, and local breweries, two of the judges, Oliver Clang and Nic Rizzo, came out the door from Main Street Coffee, a shop that rivaled Kristen's. They were smiling, as if they'd just been served a magic elixir guaranteeing them a happy life. Did they look that cheerful when drinking coffee at Roasters on the Ridge? And why wasn't Nancy with them? I assumed they were at the coffee shop as part of the contest.

I muscled into a spot farther down the block, threw the truck into park, and found my umbrella under the seat. Raindrops peppered the covering over my head as I scurried to catch up with the men, but before I could say anything, I caught Rizzo's words.

"Nancy wants to change her scores. I don't think she should be able to. Isn't there something in the rules?" Rizzo shook his head as if stumped.

"Yeah, once the form is submitted, you can't go back and adjust the ratings." Clang must've sensed me behind them, because he turned around. "Delaney?"

"Oh hi, Mr. Clang. Mr. Rizzo." I blushed under their gazes, heat creeping up my neck. I ducked further under the umbrella and cruised past them. When I reached the corner, I turned and kept walking. After circling the block, I found them gone, so I dove back into my truck and took off for the highway.

I felt like a super-sleuth catching their words like that. Was this news a clue? But a clue to what?

That Nancy wanted to change scores could only mean she wanted to redo her contest ratings. Was it Roasters' numbers she was trying to tamper with? I tried to put that worry out of my mind. Surely Nancy wouldn't do such a thing. She was mad I was asking questions, and she didn't want me talking to her ex-husband. Was she taking her displeasure out on Kristen? And Mom? What was her problem?

I was able to haul away two orange-tagged vehicles I found at ten thousand feet, both with out-of-state license plates. Even this early in the season, tourists were on the Divide encountering car trouble, as people often did at high altitude. There was nothing more satisfying than sailing along in my red tow truck with my logo on the door and a vehicle on the boom, knowing I was helping someone. I was removing cars off the dangerous roadways to a safe location. Work was a much needed distraction from whatever was going on with Nancy. And all the other thoughts tumbling around in my head. After taking the stalls to the impound lot, I sat on the frontage road waiting for calls. There was no traffic there; all was quiet. Rain streaked the windshield, and I flipped on the wipers. It was sure to be snowing again at higher elevations.

I'd brought my Murder Board with me, so I placed it on the passenger seat and studied the question that remained. There really was only one. Who killed McKenna? And I suppose I also needed to figure out why.

I wasn't about to forget her. I hadn't walked away

from the Mystery of the Woman on the Pass—as I thought of it—or my dad's mysterious death, for that matter. It wasn't right that the person who caused Dad's accident had gotten away with it. Or McKenna's killer either.

I'd turned into a crusader for justice.

A believer in punishment for the crime.

Chapter 15

Digging through the folded clothes in my dresser, I found my swimsuit at the back of the bottom drawer, shook it out, and climbed into it. Then I donned jeans and a sweater and stuffed a couple of beach towels, a tube of lip gloss, and hair clips into a tote bag.

I peeked out the window over the parking lot to check that the sun was out today and saw Ephraim's truck pull in, so I grabbed my tote, descended the steps, and jogged around to his passenger door.

"You're a few minutes early."

"I guess I'm pumped." His dimples came out to tease me.

I leaned in to give him a kiss. "Me, too. Yay! Saturday at the hot springs." Just thinking about it made butterflies take flight across my belly. He'd told me he was going to wear his racing swimsuit. With his muscles, he'd give Mr. Universe some serious competition. A flash of heat shot through my entire body at the mental image that conjured up.

After Ephraim paid for admissions, we separated at the dressing rooms. It didn't take long to disrobe down to my suit, and I took care folding my jeans and sweater into the tote bag so the clothes wouldn't be wrinkled when I put them back on. My swimsuit bottoms were high-waisted with high-cut legs in a black and white herringbone pattern. The top was a bright sunshiny yellow. Yellow flipflops with daisies protected my feet.

I realized I was hyperventilating, so I took a long breath and let it out slowly through my nose. It was now or never. After one last bracing intake of air, I stepped out to the pool area.

There was Ephraim in his naturally tanned skin.

I nearly fanned myself.

"Where are your racing briefs?" I asked, walking over.

He pointed to the leg of his baggy trunks where the famous company's logo was stitched. "I never said they'd be briefs. I guess the company makes racing trunks as well as briefs." Then his finger went to the top of my cover-all that hung to my knees and snapped the strap against my shoulder. "Is this your suit?"

"This comes off when I get in the water. But it's cold out here and I didn't want to freeze on the way in."

We gave each other broad smiles.

Ephraim laid our towels on two empty lounge chairs, and when I pulled my coverall off over my head, he said, "*Bella dama.*"

He took my hand and we slid down into the hot mineral water smelling slightly of sulfur. Ahhh...the water was warm and the air cool. His hand circled my waist. I snaked my arms around his neck and snuggled closer to him as we bobbed in the soft waves caused by the pool's jet streams. My hair floated out, surrounding us in a private cocoon. With our whole bodies nearly touching, Ephraim stared into my eyes.

Was he going to tell me he loved me? If ever there was a moment, this was it. But a comfortable silence remained between us.

"Are you relaxed?" I asked him.

He tipped his head forward in a nod. "You?"

"This water really eases the muscles." I drew back and dog-paddled in place, then sent a splash his way.

"No splashing. It's the law," he said in a stern voice before splashing me back.

After our skin was water-logged and wrinkly, we extracted ourselves from the naturally heated water and lay side-by-side on the lounge chairs, holding hands across the space between us.

I squeezed his fingers. "You're not going to talk about work?"

He turned on his side to face me, elbow bent, head resting in his palm. "Something on your mind?"

Yes. Hell, yes. But Ephraim would need to bring up the *L* word. Not me.

I said, "Any updates? Breakthroughs?"

He laughed in an intimate way. "Not really, Delaney. Do you have any?" He was as tight-lipped about his investigation as he was about his feelings.

"Wouldn't you like to know?" I teased.

He reached over and yanked our chairs closer together. I turned to face him, too, and our smiles kept breaking out into grins. As the water evaporated from our skin, we both shivered and scrambled under the towels. We soon each fell into a doze.

The sun was on the descent by the time we left the pool. Back in my jeans and Ephraim's truck, I was so mellow from the relaxing warm water that I was tempted to go back to sleep. He must've felt the same, because we stopped at a restaurant off I-70 for coffees and steak dinners.

It was a nearly perfect day.

If only Ephraim and I would DTR.

Don't even say what you're thinking. It means *define the relationship*. Remember?

Ephraim was more secretive than ever. He hadn't given me any new clues. How was I supposed to find out the identity of McKenna's boyfriend? I'd asked Kelsey and she didn't tell me either. If I pressed her for an answer, I might as well ask if she killed her sister over the boyfriend and stolen songs, too. That wasn't going to happen.

It was time to poke around elsewhere.

****

On Sunday morning I dressed in a sweater and plaid skirt. Low heels replaced my usual stilettos. There was only one Catholic church in town and Kelsey's parents were sure to be there. I planned to pump them for information, in the most sensitive way possible, of course.

Feeling like a misfit who didn't know when to stand, when to sit, and when to kneel, I stuck out in the back row like a broken flip-flop in a designer shoe store. The incense smelled strong and sacred, the singing from the balcony sounded like angels' voices, and the stained glass windows created a spectrum of heavenly colors all around. There weren't many people I recognized, and it didn't help that I could only see the backs of their heads, but Nic Rizzo caught my eye when he went to the podium. He read a passage from the Bible, what the priest referred to as the "first reading," then he took his seat and disappeared from view. The priest got up next, the same priest as the one at the cemetery, and gave a sermon. After some more readings and responses from the congregation, the priest blessed everyone, and because I was in the last pew I was first out the door.

Waiting on the front steps, I recognized Kelsey's parents from the funeral as they stopped to speak to the priest for a short spell. Then they bustled past me down the stairs toward the parking lot.

I upped my pace following them to their car. "Mrs. King? Can I talk to you?"

She turned around with raised eyebrows. "Do I know you?"

"I was at McKenna's graveside service. Do you remember me?" I didn't expect her to, not having introduced myself there. We'd never spoken.

"Of course." She was being polite.

"I'm so sorry for your loss." I brushed a strand of hair from my face. "I didn't see McKenna's boyfriend at the funeral. I hope he's all right."

"Hudson said he couldn't make it back from L.A. in time. He's a music promoter."

"Hudson?" I prompted.

"Hudson Davis."

"I only knew his first name." Because I'd heard it just now. "Is there anything I can do? I make good casseroles."

"Thank you, but we have so much food. The church has been helping with everything."

"Mary, shouldn't we be going?" Her husband tugged on her elbow. She nodded and he helped her into the car.

"Goodbye." She gave me a sad smile through the window, and I waited until their car rounded the corner before I headed back into the church to find the priest, but he was nowhere to be seen among the empty pews. I took a seat and basked in the peaceful silence. I'd give it a few minutes. Maybe the priest would return and I could talk to him about McKenna.

Nic Rizzo hustled up a side aisle and ducked into a wooden booth, shutting the door behind him. The confessional. Probably the priest was in there with him. I played a few games of free solitaire because Nic was taking a long time.

Was I being nosy by waiting for him to come out? Yes. Was being nosy a sin? I hoped not. How about playing a computer game in church? That one might be.

Rizzo finally exited the confessional, and another person materialized from nowhere and went in. Rizzo walked to the altar and dropped to his knees. This did feel intrusive now, so I looked down at my hands and wondered if I should just leave. When I looked back to the front, Rizzo was gone. He must have finished his prayers of contrition and ducked out a side door. No matter. I didn't need to speak to him. It was the priest I wanted, but he seemed too occupied, so I rose to my feet and left by the tall entry doors.

It was really worthwhile to attend church today. Kristen, of course, would say it's good to attend every Sunday, and I always meant to, but never thought about it in time. I was *sooo* glad I thought about it today.

Because I had a name, Hudson Davis.

And not only that, it was possible the judge, Nic Rizzo, knew McKenna if she came to church with her parents. That Kelsey didn't attend today did not mean McKenna didn't attend occasionally.

And what bad thing did Rizzo do that took him so long to confess?

Use your imagination. Don't you watch movies?

Once I was home, Hudson Davis's name was written

on my Murder Board mere minutes before I crossed it off.

An internet search yielded a news article and several social media posts that gave Hudson an alibi. He was at a live music event that was recorded and posted online. I'd never heard of him, but evidently he's a biggie in the music industry. This new information bolstered Kelsey's motive in my mind. I'm thinking Hudson Davis was Kelsey's boyfriend first, and according to the text I'd seen on her phone, she'd lost him to her sister. That had to hurt in more ways than one.

I was tapping my chin with my erasable marker when the phone rang with a call from Nancy Abington. What now? Had she found out I'd requested another visit with her ex-husband?

"Hello, Nancy, how can I help you?"

She said, "Delaney, you need to talk to your mom."

I sucked in a breath. "What? Why?"

"Eve stopped by my office to let me know how wonderful Kristen's coffee shop is."

"Yes, I know. Mom told me."

"I tried to tell Eve to leave it alone, but I'm not sure she got the message. It almost seemed like she was accusing me of not being fair."

It was all I could do to hold my tongue. There was so much I could bring up, like whether Nancy was trying to change her ratings. But I said, "She won't bother you again, I promise."

"Thank you." Nancy hung up.

I stared at my phone for a few moments. Was Nancy feeling guilty because she actually wasn't being fair? Did my mom hit a nerve? If Nancy had something against Roasters, how could Kris win with Nancy as a judge? I never would've believed Nancy could behave this way. It didn't make any sense. Perhaps Nancy's change of heart had to do with her hard feelings against me because I'd pressed her about her ex-husband and other things she'd rather forget. Despair parked heavily on my chest when I thought about Kristen polishing up the plaque to display her award and spending some of the award money in advance.

There was a weird dynamic going on between Nancy and her ex-husband Rob. At first Rob seemed to implicate Nancy, then he backed off. And Nancy appeared to be afraid of Rob, as if she believed he could be a killer. It was almost as if they were pointing fingers at each other. Was I caught in the middle of a divorced couple's spat? Was that all this was? Or...could Rob have caused Dad's accident? He was certainly capable. Or Nancy? Was her behavior down to a guilty conscience? If those were the only choices—and they were at the moment—then my money was on Rob.

I returned my Murder Board to the closet and lay down on my bed, clasping my hands behind my head and closing my eyes. My mind still raced as I fell into a doze.

It was dark when I woke up. Shaking off sleep, I grabbed the key to the coffee shop, which was closed on Sunday, and headed downstairs. The air outside was cool with the sun long gone. When I unlocked the door and heard it thud shut behind me, a man's voice called out, "This is the police. Stop where you are."

My skin prickled with goosebumps, but I recognized the voice before total panic set in. I squeezed my eyes shut to pull myself together. "It's just me, Zach." I marched through to the dining area, my hands up. "I'm here for a free coffee, so arrest me."

Zach stood in front of Kristen as if shielding her. "Oh, it *is* you. You don't need your hands up."

"I was joking." I gave out a half-hearted laugh and lowered my hands. "What are you two doing here?"

Kris said, "I wanted to check the register reports for the past week, and Zach came with me. You just startled us. That's all."

"Is it okay if I make myself a coffee?" Sliding past them, I went for the espresso machine.

"Of course. I already made drinks for Zach and me." The two of them leaned on the counter to watch me.

I tamped down the grounds in the basket, purged the machine, and drew the shot. The strong scent of the espresso hit my nose. Next, I frothed the milk, added it to the cup, and wiped down the wand. Before lifting the warm cup to my lips, I said, "Zach, I'm sorry you got into trouble on my account."

He waved away my concerns. "The chief only wanted to make sure there wasn't a leak from our department. It's not the city's case. It's the county sheriff's, but we share information. It's not really that big of a deal. Just procedure. But look, if you're still investigating, I want you to be careful. There's a murderer out there." I nodded, expecting more of the "quit investigating" speech or even the "don't waste police time" speech, but Zach asked, "Since we've got that settled, what have you learned?"

It took me a second to realize what he'd asked. My gaze traveled to Kristen—she gave me a quick up and down nod—then my gaze went back to Zach. "Really? You want to discuss the case?"

"Sure. What do you have?"

"I can tell you more about what I don't have. I just

haven't learned that much." I led the way to the table near the window and we all sat down. "So, this is what I know. McKenna not only stole her sister Kelsey's original songs, but she stole her sister's boyfriend, too. I believe his name is Hudson Davis, and he's a music promoter, but he has an alibi, so he's out. But Kelsey, she doesn't have an alibi, at least not one I'm aware of. And Kelsey has plenty of motive. I don't want to believe she'd kill anyone, and to look at her, well, she doesn't seem capable, but she has a pretty good reason to hate her sister."

Zach agreed. "Victims are usually killed by family or friends."

Kelsey had a big *M* on her chest, for motivation and for murder, however you want to look at it.

"But that's all circumstantial," he added.

"True that," I said. "And I have some more circumstantial evidence."

"Like what?"

"A crazed fan? McKenna had a stalker. That's why I'm considering Barlow, too. He seems the stalker type." He was definitely a crazed-fan type.

"Poor Barlow." Kristen murmured a *hmmmmm* in sympathy.

"Where did you get the information about a stalker?" Zach extracted his phone as if to make notes, probably to share with the sheriff.

I took a sip of my espresso. "Justin, one of the members of the band, told me."

A knock sounded on the front door and Tanner waved from the other side of the window. Kristen crossed over to let him in, and when he walked up to us with a big smile, I blushed. *Please make my hot face go away.* He wasn't here to see me. We'd ended our relationship a long time ago.

He said, "I was just getting back from a tow and saw you inside. Since it's Sunday and the coffee shop's closed, I was curious. I figured you're discussing the murder, being how this is strategy headquarters."

Kris said, "Actually, we *are* discussing the case."

Zach rubbed his mustache down flat against his upper lip. "Delaney was sharing what she's found out."

"I'll get you a drink, Tanner." I went behind the counter while Zach filled Tanner in on the *deets*.

I listened in when Tanner asked, "So the car wasn't dumped at the summit with the body inside?"

Zach said, "No. She drove to the scene, and she was hit on the back of the head by an unknown object. She was obviously killed while sitting behind the wheel." Tanner gave him a solemn nod.

I returned and thrust a vanilla frappé at Tanner. That was his favorite drink.

Zach glanced my way. "So, we've talked about Kelsey, Hudson, and Barlow. Do you suspect anyone else?"

I folded my arms over my chest and drummed my fingers on my elbows. "Well, I had considered the other members of the band at one time. Justin and Mace."

"What about them?"

"Anyone could tell they have a serious crush on Kelsey. McKenna looked a lot like her sister, and McKenna could sing just as well, if not better. They both claimed they didn't know McKenna, but I don't believe it. Maybe the guys had a thing for McKenna, too, not just Kelsey. Maybe one of them is the stalker."

Kristen wagged a finger. "They're friends of Axle's.

I don't think it could be one of them."

"Well, just trying to consider everybody...and..."

Zach said, "Spit it out, Delaney. I don't need to know how you found it out, but tell us what it is."

"Justin had a photo of McKenna on his cell phone. He also knew about McKenna's stalker. He obviously lied about not knowing her."

Zach had his phone out. "I've checked several criminal database apps, and I don't see a criminal history for either Mace or Justin."

I eyed his phone, trying to make out what was on the screen. How nice it would be to have access to that information.

He pulled his phone into his chest. "Don't even think about it, Delaney. I have a code that locks my phone, so forget trying to sneak a peek at it."

"Is it Kris's birthday? Is that the passcode?"

Zach eyes widened in surprise After a split second of astonished silence, he asked, "Is that everything?"

"Mace and Justin appear to have solid alibis." I pressed my fingers to my temples, my mind racing through the possible scenarios. "But I also suspect the judges, Clang and Rizzo, only because Clang seemed to resent McKenna—he called her a diva—and Rizzo may have known her from church. Not much to go on there, I admit."

Kristen's jaw dropped. "The judges? You're kidding."

Zach said, "You need to do better than that."

"I know." I sighed. "At least I eliminated a few people."

"Like who, other than Mace and Justin?"

"And the boyfriend, Hudson," Kristen interjected.

"The killer's not Axle or me or any of you." I laughed and cut my eyes to Tanner who grinned back at me.

Then his eyes darted to the window behind us and I swung around. Kristen screamed, an almost inhuman sound, and Zach's hand shot to the holster ever present on his belt.

Nic Rizzo's face was pressed to the glass.

"Oh my God." Kristen patted the place over her heart. "He startled me."

Zach clapped his hands on his knees to get up but I said, "My turn. I'll get it," and went to open the door.

Rizzo stormed into the center of the room. "Why is everyone here?"

Kris made a strangled noise so I said, "Just friends gathered together after hours? Why?"

Rizzo said, "None of you is planning to sleep here like before?"

Confusion laced Kristen's eyes and she gasped. "Before? I don't understand."

Oops. Darn it if I didn't feel my cheeks go even redder.

Rizzo gave me an accusatory look. "It's unlawful for a person to sleep in any bakeshop, kitchen, dining room, or other place where food is served." His words sounded so similar to what he'd told me before, they were probably memorized.

Zach said, "Nothing illegal is going on here, I can assure you."

Kristen shoved her chair back into the wall and shot to her feet. "I was just leaving anyway. I think we all were."

The rest of us pushed off our chairs and fell in line

as we exited the shop behind Rizzo and Kris. The men got in their trucks while Kris and I climbed the steps to our apartments.

On the landing, Kristen asked, "Did you know what that was about?"

"Yes." Embarrassment caused me to squirm. "Rizzo caught me in the coffee shop late at night once before. I wonder what his problem is. You have a right to be inside your own coffee shop."

"And you have a key, so you do, too, Delaney. Don't worry about it." But she wasn't smiling her usual smile.

Rizzo seemed to be around at the most inconvenient times. Was he spying on us? Maybe he was the stalker.

Chapter 16

So, this is what I think. The stalker is key.

At least my subconscious was telling me so.

All that night I dreamed about stalkers and woke up the next morning determined to find out who it was.

I went inside Roasters and strode right up to Guy behind the counter. "Gimme an espresso, extra hot."

He stumbled back a pace, then steadied himself.

"Please," I added.

I set up my laptop at the table in the window, and Guy delivered my espresso before hustling back behind the counter. I closed my eyes and brought to mind the photo on Justin's phone, wishing I had a print of it to fasten with the others on my Murder Board—pictures next to Boss's chew marks that I'd stared at so many times but weren't really helpful.

What was Justin's role in the sisters' lives? Why did he have their picture on his phone? Was he the stalker?

Or was it Barlow? The band called him a stalker fan, a *STAN*.

Could it be Rizzo? I had no real reason to suspect him other than he seemed to show up at weird times, like a stalker might.

If only there was a witness who could place one of them at the crime scene. The clues I had didn't prove anything.

While I was wishing for things to come, I might as well add better scene photos to my wish list. My photos and the ones from Kabir Bhatt—the man who came down the pass ahead of me—only had one perspective. The images had all been taken from the same direction.

What was on the other side of the trees? What was around the curve?

I could take another drive up the canyon to check for myself but aerial photos were easy enough to download. I opened an aerial map, zoomed in and out, rotated in a full circle, and hit the arrows to move north, south, east, and west. A structure showed up—what might be a cabin, not accessible from County Road 350 to Clarkson Pass where McKenna was found, but from another road and a different direction. The cabin didn't appear to be that far from the pass.

Could someone at the cabin have seen McKenna's Subaru Legacy? A witness? Or was it too far off? It looked like it might not be too great a distance.

No matter how hard I tried I couldn't figure out an address for the cabin. Without an address, it was beyond my capabilities to determine who owned the place. Usually I could ask my stepdad, Will, an attorney who knew his way around property records, but I needed the address.

"I brought you another espresso." Guy's words interrupted my thoughts.

"Sorry, what?"

Guy set down the fresh cup and picked up the old one. "Another espresso."

Get the heck out! Was Guy being...*nice*?

"Thanks, Guy." I made a mental note to add a five to the tip jar.

He brought his face closer to the computer screen. "What are you looking at?"

"Aerial photos of Clarkson Pass where I saw the murder victim." I waited for the snarky words, but they didn't come. I pointed to the screen. "Do you think that's a cabin?"

"Could be. But what's that?" His finger traced a line through the trees. "That's a game trail." He answered his own question.

I blew up the picture, but the distortion was too great to see anything clearly. "Can four-by-fours drive on a game trail?"

"No, I don't think so."

"What about snowmobiles?"

Both our gazes were riveted on the screen.

"I'm not even sure those can. See right there? That huge depression in the middle, it's probably a canyon. Snowmobiles can't handle that. Picture this more like a hiking trail, a difficult one. Let's check the length."

"How do you do that?"

"The 'measure distance' function." He touched the screen. "The trail's a little under three miles long." He stretched back into a stand.

"Thanks, Guy. This is helpful."

"I always try to be helpful, unlike some people I know." He shot me a look before going back to the counter where a customer was waiting.

I returned my gaze to the screen. Three miles was a far distance to be able to see anything, especially over uneven forested terrain, but this discovery still needed to be followed up.

I flopped back in my chair and stared around me. The teens at the corner table were quiet for once, nursing their coffee drinks, and I could hear the epic inspiring music playing at low volume. The antique skis and snowshoes mounted on the walls had been recently dusted. So had the distressed-wood shelves that held bags of coffee beans, mugs, and syrups.

My eyes zeroed back in on the snowshoes.

Snowmobiles couldn't traverse the game trail, but how about snowshoes? Was it possible the cabin dweller could reach Clarkson Pass from the other side by snowshoes? Could I navigate the narrow trail by snowshoes? Could I check it out? Just have a look to find out if one could see the summit from the trail or from the cabin.

I gave serious thought to what I was considering. It would take some effort. I went over my other options. There weren't any. I was at a dead end, having no more ideas, except this one.

I told myself, *I'm taking the initiative. That's what I'm doing.* It sounded so much better than interfering in a crime investigation or—*shudder*—contaminating a crime scene. I swallowed the last of my coffee, stuffed my laptop into my bag, and made a quick decision. While Guy was busy, I reached up and tugged two snowshoes off the wall and hightailed it out the door.

Preparations took about half an hour. I'd changed into a thermal top and leggings, grabbed a few items from Axle's closet, and made an assessment.

Base layer, *check*. Axle's ski pants, *check*. Axle's ski poles, *check*. Waterproof hiking boots, *check*. Binoculars, *check*. Water bottle, *check*. Sunscreen, *check*. Stolen—I mean borrowed—snowshoes, *check*. I made the final ticking-off gesture.

I filled the water bottle at the kitchen sink and made

sure my furry baby's water bowl was fresh as well. Boss took a sloppy drink, then when I grabbed my parka off the hook, he made a mad dash to the door and gazed at me with hopeful eyes.

Why not bring the big fella with me? He would love a long hike in the snow. I added a small bag of dog treats and his collapsible water bowl to my supplies.

After I fixed his leash to his collar, Boss bounded out the door and ran down the steps, tugging me behind him. He did a happy dance as he waited for me to open the passenger door.

The blue sky was sliced with thin white clouds, and the morning sun illuminated the slopes with the blinding color of diamonds. Close to the summit, the mountain vista would offer a hundred-mile view of undulating peaks covered in snow, and the peaks would soon be bald for the summer.

No driving back and forth looking for the game trail since it was marked with a signpost I'd never noticed before and not too far off from the place McKenna was left for dead. Once parked on a wide space of shoulder, I donned my gear and patted my pockets to make sure I didn't leave without my phone.

I let Boss out of the truck and he took off down the trail at a run.

"Boss!" I screamed, my voice sounding small in the wide open space.

He rushed back toward me, tail wagging.

I refastened his leash onto his collar and patted my thumping chest. I gave him the warning, "Stick with me. Don't run away and don't go too fast. I need to be able to keep up with you." At the sound of my voice, his ears perked up and he lashed his tail, and I pretended he could understand me.

The trail was well used by wildlife, trampled into a hard snowpack by the many hooves of deer and elk. We should be able to make the three-mile trip in an hour, Boss and I. I checked the time to place some sort of marker for myself. If Boss and I stuck to the trail, we wouldn't get lost. If I didn't find the cabin after an hour, we'd turn around. The trail went downhill at the beginning and would be a lot harder and take more time coming back up on the return.

After sucking in a deep frosty breath and hugging myself against the cold, I put one foot in front of the other. The smell of ice and mulch from the forest floor beneath the snow tickled my nose. At first Boss charged ahead, his leash yanking my arm, but after a while, he quit rushing forward. Plus, offering him treats kept him close to my side. Melting snow dripped from the branches of pines and twisted junipers, sometimes startling me with a loud plop. The crunching sound made by my snowshoes in the icy crust plus the smell of the Rottweiler would keep any wild animals at a distance, including bear who normally tended to avoid people.

After three-quarters of an hour, we came to the crevice seen on the aerial photo. Elk and deer hooves had carved out steps in the rock. At the bottom, a trickle of water ran under ice, the reason for game to frequent the area. The climb up the other side skirted the edge of the crevice, and the view took my breath away. Guy was correct that a snowmobile would not have been able to navigate this trail.

Boss and I both had a long drink of water at the top. Sweat trickled down my forehead, so I unzipped my parka to let in some cold air and stuffed my ski cap and gloves in a pocket. Boss's hair ruffled in the breeze and his nose twitched. He gave a whole body shiver and flicked snow all around. A few cigarette butts were captured in the icy ground and I dug them out with the toe of my boot and put them in my pocket. Such a shame someone left them.

Suddenly Boss's bark broke the stillness. He went into protective mode, on alert, and wrenched my arm as he tried to run ahead. I lifted my feet in high steps as fast as I could and held onto his leash like a jockey held onto a racehorse's reins, bouncing along after him on a path leading off the main trail.

The back side of a small but quaint log cabin came into view with a forest green metal roof and smoke puffing from the chimney.

I said, "Boss, stop, sit." And, you know what? He did.

I blew on my hands as I turned around to face Clarkson Pass. I could see a corkscrew, snake-like pattern made by the roadway above the tree line. I put the binoculars to my eyes and scanned the horizon. Not being able to tell one place from another, I lowered the binocs, but someone at the cabin might be able to pick out landmarks. Could that person have discerned a vehicle on the road? Could he or she have seen what happened to McKenna?

"Who are you?"

I did an about-face and my jaw dropped to my chest.

"Oh, Delaney, it's you." He was in a T-shirt and sweatpants with feet in untied boots that gaped open.

I untangled my tongue. "Mace? Wow. I never expected to find you here." I must've dropped the leash because Boss had his front paws on Mace's thighs, his tail wagging.

"I live here. You snowshoeing?"

I nodded.

"Come on in." Mace motioned me to follow him around to the front of the cabin. "Leave the snowshoes here."

I sank onto a bench near the door and shucked them off, my mind racing. Should I be afraid? It was a shock to find him here. This was too much of a coincidence. Could he be involved somehow? My shoulders rigid with tension, my heart pitter-pattering, I didn't quite know what to do.

"You look like you need to take a break. Follow me."

I wasn't thinking fast enough to refuse and reassured myself that he was Axle's friend after all. "All right." Sweat gathered on my chest, so I dropped my parka outside with the snowshoes and entered the cabin.

Mace left the door open a few inches, and the light from the opening landed on a brick fireplace, a rickety table, a saggy couch, and an unmade bed in a corner. The floor was concrete and the walls timber. I lowered myself onto the couch, breathed in a delicious scent of woodsmoke, and settled Boss on the floor near my feet. I worried that the beating of my heart was loud enough for him to hear.

Mace took a chair from the table, dragged it over, and straddled it backward. He crossed his arms over the chair back. "So, Delaney, why are you here?"

"I snowshoed over from Clarkson Pass. Did you know you can snowshoe from the pass to your cabin?" My voice came out an octave higher than normal.

"I know about the trail."

A nervous laugh escaped my mouth. "*Duh*. Of course, you do." My eyes darted around, taking in the skis and boots heaped in a pile by the door and the framed skiing posters that hung on the wall. "You live here. How cool is that?" I was on high-alert, yet my brain cells were still not functioning properly.

"Close to the slopes."

"Did the avalanche affect you?"

"No. I drive the other direction."

I nodded, a smile frozen in place. "Good." Boss whined and I glanced down at him. A stack of photos poked out from underneath the couch, and McKenna's printed image smiled at me. Under that one was another of both sisters.

I swallowed, my throat convulsing, and tried to calm my racing thoughts, but when I looked up I could only give Mace the thousand yard stare.

He glanced down at the photos. Suspicion must have been obvious on my face because he said, "It's not what you're thinking."

"What am I thinking?"

"That I had something to do with McKenna."

The sun glittered through the cabin's open door. Freedom was just outside. I could escape; it's not like I was trapped here. Mace didn't have me tied up like in the *Perils of Pauline*. And I could run fast in these boots without the snowshoes strapped on. Plus I had a Rottweiler with me. This was an opportunity to gather real evidence. Or was my brain stalled and I wasn't thinking clearly? What to do?

I took the risk and snatched up the photo of McKenna. "Where did you get this picture?"

His teeth were clamped together, his eyes narrowed

to slits.

"Did Justin take this picture of McKenna? Did he give it to you?"

"Yes, that's where I got it," he answered like I was giving him a lifeline.

"Both you and Justin told me you didn't know McKenna, but that was a lie, wasn't it?" I plowed recklessly on. "Which of you knew her? Both of you? Or just you, Mace? Was it you? Did you give Justin the picture of the sisters? Not the other way around?"

Mace shook his head so hard, his long hair brushed against his cheeks.

I let go of the photo, letting it fall back on the floor. "Did you harass McKenna? Were you her stalker?"

"I never harassed her. It wasn't like that." He leaned forward, gripping the back of the chair.

I was tired of the lies. The deceit. I could almost smell the bullshit.

I needed him to admit the truth.

"But it was like that. You were fascinated with McKenna. She was a phenomenal singer, even better than Kelsey, able to reach those high notes like one in a million. Not only did she have a gifted voice, she was beautiful, too, a winning combination. You hounded her, you followed her around until she told you to leave her alone."

He stared me down with dead eyes.

"But you didn't leave her alone, you kept stalking her. Kept pursuing her. You followed her everywhere." I eyed the ski equipment by the door. "You even snowshoed over to the summit."

He didn't reply except with a long steady look.

"But how did you know she'd be on the pass? Did

she agree to meet you there?"

"You have quite the imagination." He reached into a pocket and drew out a pack of cigarettes. After tapping one out, he lit it and drew in a breath. "Go on, let's hear it. Let's hear what else you can come up with."

"It's simple, not hard to picture at all. She would never agree to meet you. She wanted to avoid you, but you stood on the highway and flagged her down, forcing her off the road. Then you killed her."

He aimed a laser stare at me, and I volleyed one back until he finally said, "I know something you don't know. When I worked at L&B Garage, I repaired a car with front end damage the day after your dad's accident. Del Morran was your dad, right?"

I almost keeled over. *Holy crapoli!* "Yes."

"The car had obviously been in an accident. When the police came around asking questions about whether I'd seen any cars with damage, I didn't say anything."

A part of me scrunched up inside. "Why didn't you?" With my throat closed over, my voice was strained.

His smile was crafty. "Why should I help the police?"

"Wait." I made a fanning motion with my hands, needing to get back on course. "You're trying to distract me. I know I'm right about you. You killed McKenna, you killed her with your bare hands and left her dead body out there to be buried in the avalanche."

"No, no." He held his hands up in front of him. "It wasn't like that."

"Tell me, what was it like?" My lips trembled as I spoke. "You might as well tell me. What I can imagine would only be worse."

Boss flicked his ears back, panting at my feet. A strong, cold breeze blew in through the cracked door. My nerves were jangling, but I stabbed my fingers in Boss's hair and took a moment to calm myself. Boss wouldn't let anyone harm me. And that open door was the way of our escape.

I asked, "How did you know she'd be driving over the summit? It's pretty amazing that you would be able to figure that out."

Mace preened a little bit. "It was easy. I attached a GPS to her car, so I knew when she took the 350 exit to Clarkson Pass, right about the time my package was delivered. I did use the snowshoes. After the delivery guy left, I snowshoed over as fast as I could. I barely got there in time, but she saw me and stopped her car. The big snow hadn't hit yet."

Attaching a GPS to someone's vehicle sounded like criminal-level stalking behavior to me. How I wished McKenna hadn't stopped. Why did she? If only she hadn't. I hung my head down, and the picture of her with her sister stared up at me. I raised my chin. "How did Kelsey play into this?"

"What do you mean? They didn't even speak to each other anymore. They had a fight over that creep, Hudson, and Kelsey accused McKenna of stealing her songs."

"Why would Kelsey sing in your band, Mace? Didn't she know you were McKenna's stalker?" I tried to make sense out of it.

"I was not a stalker." He pronounced the words slow and loud, then took a last drag and threw his cigarette on the concrete floor. "I loved her, but McKenna never told her sister about me. I wasn't important enough." The little bit of pride I'd seen on his face a moment ago morphed into something else…embarrassment?

"She did tell her, just not your name. She told her about a man who--"

"I was not a stalker." He spoke in glacial tones. His cold words, and the frosty air that raced through the open door, slapped my face for a wake-me-up.

It was time to do something. To hatch that escape plan.

I said, trying to appease him, "I believe you."

"No, you don't."

"I do, I do."

He stood up and his chair fell over. He shook his head, like *he* didn't believe *me*. *Jeez*, didn't anyone trust my words?

Of course, I was lying this time. We both were, and we both knew it.

His long legs carried him across the room where he slammed the door shut. He turned to face me, his hands fisted, his eyes bulging.

It was past time to do something.

Chapter 17

"Boss! Attack!" I nudged him. "Boss!"

Tongue lolling, he turned over onto his back as if asking for a tummy rub. "Boss! Attack!" His tail drummed the floor. I thought Rottweilers were supposed to be aggressive. This one was the epitome of calm.

Me? I wasn't calm.

I jumped into a wide-legged stance, then ran straight for Mace. I kicked up one leg with my well-toned calf and gave him a powerful kick where it hurts. Thank God for all those squats over the tow dollies.

He crumpled to the floor, his face a picture. And it wasn't a pretty one.

I threw open the door and ran out like I was being chased by a hungry bear. I wasn't thinking straight, I was panicked. The toe of my boot caught on the stoop and I did a face plant in the snow. I rose to my hands and knees. Axle's ski pants were torn, both of my hands were scraped, and my teeth were chattering.

Mace must have recovered because he barreled out the door, and not expecting me on the ground, performed a long jump over my head. He somersaulted over me, coming to rest a few feet away. I felt around for a weapon and my hand landed on one of my snowshoes.

We both groped our way to a stand, and I wielded the snowshoe out like a weapon. "Don't come any closer."

"Be careful. You can really hurt someone with that."
He bared his teeth.

We were surrounded by a forest of trees. The air
smelled like growing things stirring under the dirt.
Mace's rusty VW van that held the band's equipment sat
in a frozen and weedy dirt driveway. It was eerily quiet.

I hefted up the snowshoe, feeling the weight of it.
"Is that how you killed McKenna? With a snowshoe?"

Before I could react, he'd scooped up the other one.
We were at a standoff, circling each other with dueling
snowshoes.

He pushed his chest out, and the veins in his neck
throbbed. "She didn't even get out of her car. She was
going to drive off. She was getting ready to pull out, and
she stuck her head out the window to look over her left
shoulder. She'd twisted herself around in her seat, and
I…I just backhanded her on the head with my snowshoe.
I didn't mean to hurt her, honestly. I just wanted to stop
her from leaving. But she fell back into her seat and I
realized she was dead."

"You left her there. You had time to get back to the
cabin and drive into town for band practice."

"Yes," he admitted. "It had started to snow really
hard but I made it."

He'd just provided me his means, motive, and
opportunity. He'd probably figured he might as well fess
up. After all, who was I going to tell after he killed me?
I knew he planned to, from the manic glint in his eye.

A loud *GRRRR-GRRR-GRROOOWWWL* sounded
from behind us.

A bear?

No. It couldn't be.

I couldn't have that kind of bad luck, could I? To confront a killer, only to be gobbled up by a bear? Instead of my life passing before my eyes, the video of the bear I towed flashed across my mind, and I even had a microsecond to wonder if the animal had been relocated here.

A black and brown mass launched into the air, soaring, soaring, front legs out, back legs stretched behind, landing on Mace with a whump. I screamed until the breath went out of my lungs.

It was Boss. He did attack. He was just a little slow on the uptake. I watched, spellbound, heart banging in my chest, while Boss nailed the killer to the ground.

The sound of tires approaching caused me to spin toward the road. A black and white police car careened to a stop and Zach jumped out. "Are you all right, Delaney?"

"Yes, yes." I pointed at Mace. "He's the killer. He killed McKenna. Quick, don't let him get away." I fluttered around, as nervous as a quaking aspen, while Zach cuffed Mace and brought him to a stand. Boss backed off and sat on his haunches.

The officer muscled Mace over to the bench and sat him down. "Well, tell me." Zach rested his hands on his duty belt.

My voice only cracked a little as I explained how Mace snowshoed over the game trail and killed McKenna by hitting her on the back of the head with one of his snowshoes. Mace gazed into the distance, back to his brooding self. When I was done, a sense of accomplishment washed over me.

I asked, "But why are you here, Zach? Did you figure out Mace was the murderer? Is that why you showed up?"

The Spruce Ridge officer looked tired and drawn. "Let me secure Mr. Mason in the police car and call this in, then I'll tell you about it." Zach frog-marched Mace to the cruiser's backseat. The *Rottie* leaned into my hand and enjoyed the ear scrunches while we waited for Zach to get off the radio. His long leash had come loose from his collar, so I picked it up. He seemed too interested in all the excitement to run away.

Zach finished talking on his mic and came back over to me. "Okay. Backup is on the way. Let me tell you what happened. Axle got home and found his dog missing. He tried to call you, but you must've been out of cell range. You should've left him a note, Delaney."

My cheeks warmed. "Oops. Forgot."

"So Axle got together with Kris, and they checked the GPS on Boss's collar, and Kristen sent me the coordinates. We knew Albert Mason lived here. He'd been questioned by the sheriff's department and cleared."

"Albert?"

"We put two-and-two together and figured you came up here and brought Axle's dog with you. I thought you and Mason must be friends. I had no idea you were in danger, but then Kristen caught me on the phone right before I got here to let me know that Guy had seen you looking at aerial photos around Clarkson Pass. Guy told us about the game trail. Then, when I pulled in the driveway, I saw Boss take that flying leap." He threw his arms up in the air. "When are you going to keep out of trouble? When are you going to stay safe?"

"Never?" I hazarded a guess. "So, you didn't know Mace was the murderer?"

He shook his head. "I would've brought back-up

with me and not have had to call for it."

"Zach, I didn't know either. I only just put it together. And that's what I'm going to tell the sheriff. You're the one who found me and showed up at the right time."

He circled a finger around his collar. "You didn't guess from your Murder Board?"

"Not really. And about that…someone provided the news editor a picture of my Murder Board, and he posted it online. I'll bet Mace took that photo. I'm not sure why he'd give to Clang, though."

"I'll interrogate Oliver Clang and find out where he was getting his information. It's possible Mason was feeding him stories to discredit you and point the suspicion away from himself."

"You said Mace was questioned and released?"

"He was, but he was probably still worried that he'd be caught. He told the detective he was here the whole day until he drove into town for band practice. He didn't take Clarkson Pass into town, of course, because the way down from here is on County Road 310, not 350. We didn't think about the game trail." Zach pinched the corner of his mustache between his thumb and index finger. "We didn't know to check his snow equipment. We'll look for his snowshoes and test them for blood and tissue residue."

I gagged a little in the back of my throat. "There's ski equipment inside the cabin, or the snowshoes might be in the van in the driveway. I've seen skis and stuff back there. Can Boss and I get a ride with you to my truck?"

"Of course. My back-up officer can take you."

Yay me! Yay Boss! We didn't have to take the game

trail back. We rode in luxury in a police car, then followed the officer down to the sheriff's station.

The officer sped a little above the limit and I did, too, to keep up. At the station, I texted Axle while I was waiting for my turn to be questioned, Boss at my side, and my li'l cuz shot me some serious side-eye when he came in for his dog. I wanted to lie down across the uncomfortable chairs, I was so exhausted. It felt like I had to wait forever. At one point Oliver Clang walked in. He checked at the intake desk, then he was allowed through to the back.

Finally, I was taken into an interrogation room where I spent the next couple of hours, but not with Ephraim. It was with another detective. Something about a conflict of interest. By the time I was allowed to leave I was utterly beat, but when I ran into Ephraim in the hall, I perked up.

The sheriff gave me a thorough inspection. "Are you all right?"

The adrenaline had wound down, but still I had to take a quaky breath. "I'm fine."

He took my hand and led me back to his office. "I have some news."

"Did Mace confess?"

"Not entirely. He started to tell us about your dad's accident. He was trying to use the information as a bargaining tool to negotiate a plea."

"He told me he repaired a car that looked like it was in an accident around the time of Dad's hit and run. Nancy Abington told me the same thing."

"You should have come to me with that information. Anyway, Mason went one step further. He said he'd testify against Rob Abington for a deal. He said

Abington gave him the keys and told him to run your dad off the road. Abington was worried your dad was going to the police with information about the chop shop."

"Mace killed my dad?" I was too tired to be surprised. Or maybe I wasn't really surprised at all.

"He claimed he didn't mean for the accident to be fatal, but then he lawyered up. We won't get any more information out of him now." He held my hand across the desk. "I think we can get a conviction with what we have."

Ephraim briefed me about Clang's interrogation, but my mind was still spinning with thoughts of my dad's accident. I'd always wondered why Dad didn't try to see me when I was growing up. It was a mystery as to why he left me his tow truck. I never got to know him well enough to understand why he did what he did. At least the mystery of his hit and run was solved. I could put that question to rest.

****

Spring had definitely arrived the next morning. It was the last day the ski resort was to remain open, and skiers showed up at Roasters wearing swimsuits and tutus, an unofficial closing day tradition. The sun and the exertion of the sport would keep the skiers warm. When the crowd thinned, Kristen and Guy joined Axle, me, and my Murder Board at the table in front.

Kristen said, "Zach told me Mace was involved in your dad's hit-and-run accident. I can hardly believe it of him. How are you doing with this news, Delaney? Are you okay?"

"It's good to finally know the truth," I answered, blinking rapidly. Everyone remained silent for a beat. Kris grabbed my hand and gave it a squeeze.

Guy asked, "So, Mace was driving the hit-and-run car in your dad's accident?"

I explained, "Mace told Ephraim that Rob Abington put him up to running my dad off the road. Rob thought my dad was going to tell the police what he knew about the chop shop Rob was running at L&B Garage."

Axle's eyes were round and his shoulders hunched up to his ears. "I had no idea about Mace, Delaney. Honest, I didn't."

"Of course not." I rubbed the tears away and gave him playful shoulder bump. "I didn't think you did."

"There was a lot more going on at L&B than I knew about." Axle made a small side-to-side movement with his head. "I should've guessed about the chop shop."

"I'll agree with you there." I twisted his ear.

"Ouch!" He gave me a punch in the arm.

Guy asked, "So, Mace not only ran your dad off the road, he bashed McKenna over the head, too?"

I was still processing everything and not yet feeling the reality of it. "I guess if you caused one person's death, the second time is easier." I pointed to the suspect list I'd written on the Murder Board. "Here, I thought Justin was the more likely suspect."

Axle's eyebrows rose in a question. "Why was Justin more likely?"

"I didn't get a chance to tell you about the photo of McKenna and Kelsey I saw on Justin's phone. I thought he'd lied about knowing McKenna. But Mace was the one who'd taken that picture before the sisters had their blowup. He was stalking McKenna and snapping her picture without her knowing. He explained to Ephraim, who told me, that he'd sent it to Justin by mistake with a bunch of photos of the band Justin wanted to use for marketing."

"When did you suspect Mace?" Kristen asked.

"Not until I found him at the cabin. Really, it was just before Zach showed up."

Guy asked me, "Weren't you concerned about confronting Mace if you thought he was the killer?"

"Of course, but I wasn't going to let that keep me from asking questions. Plus, I had Boss with me." He'd turned out to be my protector after all.

"So…what was up with Oliver Clang? Zach said he'd been brought in for questioning, too," Kristen said.

"He was. Ephraim told me that Clang knew my reputation for solving crimes and thought I suspected *him* of the murder. He thought I was staring at him all the time, but I was just staring at his ugly orange shoes. He's uber paranoid and always spouting crazy conspiracy theories. He started posting stories to discredit me, and Mace was helping him."

Axle said, "And how better to make you look ridiculous than with the bear video?" The drum riff he performed in the air with his drumsticks looked complicated.

I pressed my lips together and didn't even bring up how snare-noxious Axle was. I said, "Clang didn't know someone would read the news reports and take up taunting me with graffiti. That was an added bonus in his mind."

"I know who painted the graffiti and I already talked to them," Kris said. "It was those teens who are always here. They come in for coffees every day."

"Why would they tag the shop if they love the place so much?" They were probably the ones who'd soaped my car and yelled, "Stilettos kick ass," from the Dodge

Charger, too.

"Why do teens do anything they do?" Kristen looked at Axle, who tossed a drumstick up in the air, but missed the catch when it dropped to the floor.

"Well, you did suspect Clang, so maybe he wasn't that paranoid." Guy pointed a finger at the board. "There's his name on your list."

"He's one obsessed guy, trust me." I tugged on my braid. "What I don't understand is…why you were mad at me, Guy."

He said, "Only because you were blowing Kristen's chances to win the contest."

Kristen's head jerked up to look at her barista. "Oh, no. You were mad at Delaney?" She tsked. "Delaney is nothing but good and kind."

We all glanced at her in astonishment. But, hey, I'll take it.

"Well, I don't need this anymore." I set the board on the floor.

Kris said, "Zach's warning has been deleted from his work record. He even got a commendation, Delaney. Thanks for putting in a good word for him."

"Just telling it like it is. I'm glad he showed up when he did. Boss could only hold onto Mace for so long." I turned to Axle. "What did the vet say when you had Boss checked out?"

My li'l cuz was so upset by Boss's ordeal, he'd taken his dog to the vet. Axle answered, "He said Boss tries to escape the apartment because he's bored and needs more walks."

I could understand that since I was often bored myself. Maybe instead of playing solitaire all the time, I'd take Boss for runs at the park. I tapped the icon on my phone to delete the app. No more card games.

As soon as everyone left, I ordered a caramel macchiato to go, climbed into my Fiat, and headed over to Abington Auto Store. McKenna King's murder was solved. But unanswered questions remained about Dad, and I was still trying to fit the information I'd learned into what I already knew.

"This is for you." I plonked the hot drink on Nancy's desk. "And we need to talk."

"Is this about the contest? I did not change Kristen's scores...or anyone else's." For a moment she looked guilty, though.

I eased into the chair across from her. "That's not why I'm here. You heard Mace, that is, Albert Mason, was the one who killed the girl on Clarkson Pass?"

"I did." She plumped back in her chair. "I heard you solved another murder."

I blurted out the whole story, and ended with, "Did you know Mason was the driver of the hit-and-run vehicle? He used to work at L&B Garage."

"No." Her face went white.

"I'm not sure I believe you, Nancy."

For a second, it looked like her eyes flashed with shock, then her gaze went cold. "What are you trying to say?"

"You knew, didn't you?" Tears pressed at my eyes.

"Are you crazy? Quit talking nonsense."

Water welled up in my eyes, about to spill over. She opened her mouth as if she was going to argue, then her features softened and she nudged the tissue box on her desk closer to me. "Do you really believe I knew who ran Del off the road? Really, Delaney?"

I sniffed and scraped my nose across my sleeve. "I

don't want to believe it. But I think you've been lying to me, steering me in wrong directions."

She averted her gaze, then picked up the to-go cup. "I knew that Rob asked one of the kids at the garage to run Del off the road as a warning. I overheard him talking on the phone. I didn't know who he was talking to. I heard the next morning that the accident was fatal. Rob said I couldn't go to the police, that it was too late and I'd be charged with aiding and abetting because I was present when he made the call." Her voice was low. I could barely hear her.

"Did you know Mace?"

"I knew who he was. I knew him from the garage. But I didn't suspect it was him. Mace only seemed to care about his music and his skiing. He never said anything to me. But Delaney, it feels good to get it off my chest. I like you. I never meant to hurt you or your dad. I'm sorry. I have these terrible regrets for holding back. I only cared about what people thought of me, about my success in the business, and now I know those things don't really matter. Delaney, you are on top of the world, you are a success, you have your own business, you have friends and family. And if you have someone you love who loves you and believes in you too, well, that is success. Be happy."

"I am happy." I realized how right she was. "But you need to talk to the police." I handed her my phone. "This is the sheriff's number."

I sat in her office looking out the window while she called. I could hear Ephraim's voice asking her questions, and her responses went on for some time. Light snowflakes filled the sky for one last snowfall of the season.

Nancy disconnected and passed my phone back to me. "Ephraim's on his way over."

I knuckled my eye to scrub away tears, hating that my emotions were so close to the surface. "Thanks for stepping up. I'd better get going. He'll want to talk to you on his own."

"See you later, Delaney." Her words floated after me as I took off down the hall.

Once back in my car, I let my thoughts gather.

Rob Abington had been sentenced to prison for running a chop shop at L&B Garage. Before his arrest he'd admitted Dad had known and confronted him about his criminal activities. He hinted that Dad's death was somehow a result of that angry exchange. I'd anguished over Dad's death for a long time, worried he was somehow caught up in illegal activities. But he hadn't been, and for that I was grateful. I'd always known Rob was involved, but I was still reeling from the news that Mace was the driver. If Nancy had gone to the police right away, would it have helped me get past my dad's death sooner? Why had Rob pointed me in the right direction, to Nancy? Maybe he felt guilty and wanted the truth to come out. I'll still never know Dad, I'll still question what might have been if he had lived, but at least I have justice for Dad now. And for McKenna.

****

I don't know how many times I was stopped in my truck or in the coffee shop by folks asking how I was doing and wanting to buy me a coffee. My phone rang off the hook with calls from concerned friends. I didn't realize I knew so many people in town or that they knew me. The buzz finally wound down, and since the awards ceremony for the restaurant contest was coming up, speculation as to which restaurant won took over the topic of conversation. We were getting quite excited to find out. I kept busy working the towaway zones and cruising the interstate for breakdowns, and when my cellphone rang one more time, I answered it, hoping for a tow. Getting back to normalcy would be a relief.

"Delaney Morran?" a woman asked.

"Yes, that's me. Del's Towing."

"Oh, good. You might not remember me. Shari Bannock? You towed my Tesla from the mall to a mechanic's shop down the street. Do you recall that?"

How could I forget? She'd filmed the whole thing.

"Of course. You posted a video. It was very nice, thanks." I did like the positive publicity.

"I'd like to talk to you about that. Do you have time to meet with me? I'll be in Spruce Ridge tomorrow."

"What's it about?"

"I'd prefer to talk in person. Can you meet me at Spruce Ridge Legal Practice on Main Street?"

I gulped. "Do I need a lawyer?"

"Actually, you might want to bring one." She laughed, but I didn't see any humor in the situation.

Fighting the panic gripping my chest, I dialed up my stepdad, Will.

I'd given the Tesla owner, Shari Bannock, permission to film, but not to post. If anyone was going to sue anyone, it was me who should be doing the suing.

When Will answered and I explained everything, he said he would run a background check on Shari Bannock and that he would attend the meeting with me the next day. He asked, "Are you all right, Delaney? With everything you've been through?"

Will and Mom had driven up to Spruce Ridge to be

with me the night Mace was arrested. I'd assured them I was fine then, and I assured Will again now.

But, to be honest, I wasn't fine. I was shaky and scared. It seemed I had one more thing to come to terms with. I just didn't know what it was.

Chapter 18

At first I thought the next day wouldn't come soon enough, then I thought it had come too fast. I dressed in a black skirt and jacket and black heels—black for professional and also for grim—and met Will on the corner of Pine and Main Street. We walked the block to the law office together.

Will said, "Shari Bannock is the marketing director for a designer shoe company. The business has been involved in lawsuits, but only in patent cases, nothing that would involve you. I called the company's legal department, but they put me off, saying all would be explained at the meeting today."

I gripped his arm. "What do you think it could be?"

"I have no idea, but you haven't done anything wrong." Will gave me a reassuring smile. "People get alarmed whenever attorneys are involved. It's the lawyer syndrome." We'd reached the door to the historic building, and he held it open for me.

We stepped into a small lobby with dark wood paneling, book-lined walls, and an ancient receptionist with a gray-haired bun, like out of an old movie set. Will introduced us, and the elderly woman opened a heavy wooden door that led to a small conference room. Shari Bannock sat at a mini-sized library table next to a suited man.

"Delaney, I'm so glad to see you again." She looked happy, not threatening. I took the seat opposite her and introduced Will Sharpton as my lawyer. She didn't need to know he was family.

She introduced the suited man next to her as the attorney for the shoe company. His chubby neck looked pinched in his tight collar and tie. He slid a stack of papers across the table in my direction. I glanced at Will, and he took hold of the papers.

"We'd like to offer you a contract to represent our shoe company." Shari turned a hopeful gaze on me. "All that is required is for you to wear our shoes while out on tows and post photos and videos on social media. In exchange, you will receive a small stipend for each post, plus our newest shoe samples. I'll need your size."

I was speechless and could tell a flush started at my neckline. This was nothing like I'd expected. But what had I expected? Never once had I imagined this.

Will said, "We'd like to read over the contract and get back to you. Do you have a deadline?"

"It's in the contract," the company lawyer answered. "By the end of the month, April 30."

Will nodded and motioned to me that we should leave. As I stood, I finally found my voice. "Why me? I'm just curious."

Her lips turned up in a delighted smile. "I had over thirty thousand hits on my video of you towing in heels. And your bear video, that was hilarious! Even better, the video of you lip-synching with some band."

My mouth gaped open in astonishment. I didn't know Barlow had posted the lip-synching video.

"And then you made the news again when that Spruce Ridge police officer showed up to save you from a killer. You're a gold mine."

Will propelled me by the elbow. "We'll have no problem meeting your deadline." He ushered me through the dark lobby and out the door. He said, "Don't say anything yet. Let's talk at the car."

Once we stopped at his driver's door, I hardly heard his advice. Something about looking over the contract...considering a counter offer...and blah blah blah.

I couldn't keep the shocked expression off my face, but I did manage to ask, "Why negotiate? I'm lucky to get this offer."

"Let me go through the documents first. I'll call you."

I thought about that. "Okay, fair enough."

It was too hard to move on from this exciting prospect to the boring monotony of policing the towaway zones and searching for broken-down vehicles. Too much had happened, and I was feeling a bit fragile. So I paced the apartment, phone in hand. It took Will two long hours to let me know the contract was fair and valid. I signed it electronically, without any negotiation, and Will returned it to the shoe company.

OMG!

So, it's not like I'm going to get rich. The biggest bonus was the shoes. But still. Me, the badass high-heeled tow truck driver...I was going places. Maybe I could buy a new flatbed and hire a second driver after all. Someday.

Then, I snapped back to reality. This was me we're talking about. Could it be real?

Jussayin.

Once my phone pinged with Will's confirmation

that it was a done deal, I thundered down the stairs and threw open the door to Roasters on the Ridge. Bursting inside, I entered into the warm, moist heat that smelled like cinnamon and strong coffee…like home. Nothing smelled more comforting than my best friend's latest batch.

Kristen was buttoned up with customers, Axle was packing his drum kit into cases, and Guy was bussing tables. The snowshoes I'd borrowed were back in their usual place on the wall. The enormity of everything that had happened hit me, and I collapsed onto a nearby chair. Guy made his way to my table and spritzed the top with vinegar water.

He said, "Oh, you're here. Did you hear the news?" at the same time I said, "I've got news."

Guy said, "You first."

I said, "No, you."

"The restaurant contest was called off." He waited a mo while my eyebrows shot up in surprise. "Nic Rizzo was disqualified."

"Rizzo? But, I thought Clang was the one in trouble. Clang was the one questioned by the police."

"He was disqualified, too."

"I'm confused." I pinched the bridge of my nose. "How's this possible?"

"Rizzo's with the Health Department."

I said, "Yeah, yeah, I know."

"He was taking bribes to overlook health violations," Guy explained. "He was removed from the judging panel when the contest organizers found out."

I mulled that over. It might explain why Rizzo showed up after hours with silly threats. "What about Clang?"

"He was exposed as a conspiracist. One too many of his theories was debunked. He got kicked out of the news association, so he was removed from the judges' panel, too."

"Wow. He really fell off the edge."

"There's more." He pressed his lips together, straightened up, and shoved his hands onto his hips. "This is where it gets weird."

With a cymbal in his hands, Axle stopped on his way to the door. "How can it get any weirder? It's already at quantum fail."

Guy dipped his head in agreement. "The mystery judge was revealed. Barlow! Barlow Harmen. He's a food blogger. Who knew?"

"But he's Kelsey's stalker." I figured it had to be him since Mace was stalking McKenna, not Kelsey, and everyone else was eliminated. Barlow was the only one left. And the logical one, too.

"He was never a stalker. Kelsey had nothing to fear. Barlow was always around because he was checking out the restaurants."

"What?"

"No way."

Axle and I spoke at the same time.

Kris handed off drinks to her last two customers and rushed over to us.

"You heard the news?" Her face was red, her jaws were clenched, and her fists shook. "What was the city thinking, appointing those judges? First Rizzo's thrown off the judges' panel, then Clang. It's insane." Kristen's cheeks puffed out, and her voice had risen to shriek level.

Axle and I both did a double-take. Axle said in an undertone, "Now we know what Kristen looks like when she loses it."

I jumped to her side. "Don't be upset. Just relax. It'll all be fine."

Her face turned from red to scarlet and she thrashed her arms through the air like a giant inflatable tube man. "All that work, a new roaster, upping my marketing plan, my staff going the extra mile, and for what? The contest was called off until next year. There aren't going to be any winners this year."

Patting her arm, I said, "Kris, the good news is, you didn't lose. Look on the bright side."

Kris threw off my hand, stormed across the room, and ripped the empty plaque from the wall. She tossed it in the trash can and dusted her hands together. "There."

Axle said, "At least she didn't try to flush it down the toilet."

She drew in a deep breath and held it, puffing out her cheeks even more.

Was she going to scream? Was she going to hold her breath until she passed out? This was not how my best friend typically behaved. She never went into a tirade. Never, ever. For a long interval all was silent, and the silence was so absolute, not one of us seemed to be breathing.

A sheen of perspiration broke out on Guy's forehead.

Axle looked too queasy to speak.

And me? I had an apple-sized lump in my throat.

I finally said, "It'll all work out. You'll see. Everything works out for the best. You'll get through this. Uhhh..." I had nothing else.

"Good heavens, you sound just like me, Delaney." Kris let out a long laugh, ending on a hiccup. "Now I know how *you* feel. I'll stop repeating all those platitudes, I promise."

We all exhaled a collective sigh of relief.

"Kris, you're such a great encourager and I know you mean well…and I like how calm and collected you always are. I mean, how you *normally* are." But I hated that I was usually the one on the receiving end of those platitudes. "And it's okay to have righteous indignation. It's okay to get mad." And that was good advice to me, too. Maybe a little righteous anger toward Rob and Mace, and even Nancy, was just what I needed toward that last step of closure. Except I wasn't angry, I just realized. I was happy, not mad. All the mysteries solved.

Kris said, "Byron told me the contest doesn't really matter. I should've listened to him. I was making way, way too much of it. I'm glad it's over."

Axle set down the cymbal and fished the plaque from the trash. He rubbed his sleeve across the wood face and handed it back to her. "For next year. You know by then you'll feel like entering the contest again."

"Thanks, Axle." Kris gave him a big smile, then turned to me. "Can you believe this, Delaney? I didn't win the contest—"

"Nobody won," I interrupted.

"—and Axle's band broke up."

He jumped in. "Yeah, Kelsey's gone for good. Off to L.A. with her old boyfriend, Hudson."

"—but you solved the crime, Delaney. You actually did what you set out to do." Kristen pressed a hand over her heart.

Guy let out a disbelieving snort. "What a role reversal."

Should I be offended? I gave him my best what-the-hell glare.

I said, "You'll win next year, Kris. And you'll form an even better band, Axle." I turned to Kris. "But how are you going to pay for your new roaster without the award money?"

"I had that covered. You weren't worried, were you? I hope you know me better than that. But I won't be able to add an online store like I was planning. Not yet anyway."

Axle said, all thoughts still on himself, "The talent scout never showed up to see the band. Like in *Waiting for Guffman*. Probably for the best. Now that the band's not practicing as much, I can go out with you on tows."

"Really, Ax?" I gave him a side-hug. "That'd be great. You know, just until you get busy again." Was now the time to bring up my good news? Or would that be rubbing it in? Should I just drop it for now? I didn't need to be the center of attention. In fact, I didn't want to be.

As if he could read my thoughts Guy asked, "So, what's your news? You said you had news."

"It's nothing." I flapped my hand.

"What is it?" Kristen said.

Axle said, "Come on. Spill."

"Well…brace yourselves." I lifted a palm in a wait-for-it gesture. "I just signed a contract with a shoe company to promote their merchandise. I get free shoes." I did a little dance across the floor. That might be the best part of the whole arrangement.

"No way," Axle said.

"Really?" Kris's eyebrows elevated in a question.

I straightened up to my full height—such as it was—and set my jaw in a hard line. "Why doesn't anyone ever believe me?"

"What, it's true?" Kristen's gray eyes lit up.

"Yes." I blew a sigh.

"That's so *slay*." Axle punched me in the arm, then we slapped high fives.

"Yeah, great," Guy said with a marked lack of enthusiasm.

"That's wonderful. I'm making free drinks for everyone." Kristen turned on her heel to head toward the espresso machine. Soon, she was handing drinks around, smiling at the customers.

****

So here I was, back in my truck. The rain shimmered on the pavement. Rain, not snow, thank goodness. The chokecherry trees perfumed the air with their light pink blossoms, and the cool rain made me glad for my hoodie. Rain was good in Colorado. It filled the reservoirs and kept us from droughts.

Ephraim pulled his Chevy Silverado with Sheriff - Clear Creek County next to my truck. We both got out into a fine mist.

The sheriff scooted in close and his cowboy hat shielded both our faces. "I see you have on a new pair of shoes."

I bent my knee to draw up my foot and examine the awesome clogs with snow globes for heels. This cutting-edge design was worn by celebrities…and me, now.

"You like them?" I laughed in what I thought was a flirtatious way and tried to bat my eyelashes.

"They're…different." He brushed my hair aside to put his hand on the back of my neck and draw me into a kiss.

My lips still burning, I cast my eyes down and

242

asked, "You like my shoes as much as you like me?"

"No, I love you." He laughed. "Don't love the shoes so much." He pulled back as if waiting for my reaction.

I forced my eyes to meet his. "You love me?" What, is this it? The DTR moment?

"Yes, *mi amor*, I love you."

Melting inside, I said, "I love you, too." A drop of rain splashed on my face and cooled my heated cheeks.

He opened my truck door for me and I climbed inside. I flashed him a happy grin through the open window.

He walked backwards toward his truck, his cowboy boots clopping on the payment. He called out, "There's absolutely no one else in the whole world like you, Delaney."

"Are you sure about that?" I hollered back.

He slid into his truck and waved his cowboy hat out the window. "You're unique. One of a kind."

That's me.

The shoeaholic tow truck driver.

A word about the author...

Karen C. Whalen is the author of two mystery series: the Dinner Club Mysteries featuring Jane Marsh, an empty nester who hosts a gourmet dinner club, and the Tow Truck Mysteries starring Delaney Morran, a super feminine shoe-a-holic who drives a tow truck. Both are cozy mysteries about strong friendships and family ties set in Colorado. The first book in the Dinner Club series tied for First Place in the Suspense Novel category of the 2017 IDA Contest sponsored by Oklahoma Romance Writers of America. In the Tow Truck series, Eyes on the Road was a Second Place winner of the 2023 Firebird Book Awards in the Cozy Mystery category. Whalen worked for many years as a paralegal at a law firm in Denver, Colorado and was a columnist and regular contributor to The National Paralegal Reporter magazine. Whalen loves to host dinner parties, entertain friends, ride bicycles, hike in the mountains, walk on the beach, and read cozy murder mysteries.